THE UNLOVED

THE UNLOVED

Deborah Levy

BLOOMSBURY

NEW YORK • LONDON • NEW DELHI • SYDNEY

Published by Bloomsbury USA, New York
Bloomsbury is a trademark of Bloomsbury Publishing Plc

All papers used by Bloomsbury USA are natural, recyclable products made from wood grown in well-managed forests. The manufacturing processes conform to the environmental regulations of the country of origin.

LIBRARY OF CONGRESS CATALOGING-IN-PUBLICATION DATA HAS BEEN APPLIED FOR.

ISBN: 978-1-62040-677-9

First published by Jonathan Cape 1994
First U.S. edition published 2014
This paperback edition published 2015

1 3 5 7 9 10 8 6 4 2

Typeset by Jouve (UK), Milton Keynes
Printed and bound in the U.S.A. by Thomson-Shore Inc., Dexter, Michigan

Bloomsbury books may be purchased for business or promotional use. For information on bulk purchases please contact Macmillan Corporate and Premium Sales Department at specialmarkets@macmillan.com.

PART ONE

I know who killed her, says Tatiana the unloved child.

Detective Inspector Blanc stares dreamily into the pink folds of the child's taffeta dress. A gold paper crown sits askew on her unwashed hair. 'Who was it, Princess?' He tries to make his voice careless.

Tatiana smiles flirtatiously and taps his shoulder with her silver wand. Glitter falls from her stick and stains the navy serge of his jacket. 'Biddy Ba Ba,' she screams, pointing to the cat asleep on the chair. When she runs into the reluctant arms of her mother the Detective Inspector wants to murder her.

Be calm. Be patient, he tells himself, drinking the last dregs of the bitter coffee the bohemian tourists in the château have made for him. He gathers his papers and stands up. Tatiana's mother looks bored. Inspector Blanc stares hard at the small black pearls, the caviar that circles her milky neck. The exquisite sculpture of her shoulders. The snail of gold hair that has slithered out of her chignon and rests on the slope of her neck. How did this jewel, this perfection, this poised and perfumed woman spawn such an ugly child? When she looks down at her daughter's feet, he could swear her eyelids are powdered with silver dust. She is a mask, he muses, all artifice – as if somehow keeping mortality at bay. She is eternity, she is Chanel, she is Dior, she is Guerlain. She is quite simply perfect. A synthetic illusion painted with her own brush. Her narrow silhouette and the nuggets of antique silver on her wrists fascinate and perturb him. But the little girl? He'd show the princess the back of his hand and make her yelp.

The Inspector's shoes press angrily into the gravel path as he walks to his car.

'Don't tell lies.' Luciana stares impassively at the wall as the eleven-year-old girl struggles out of the froth of pink lace and chiffon which is too small for her. The zip does not quite do up and she has to squeeze the princess dress over her plump hips. Dropping it at her mother's feet she thuds upstairs to her bedroom and bursts into tears.

Luciana fastens the small tortoiseshell button on her linen cuff. Serene and symmetrical down to the two detailed pleats in her faded tea rose linen skirt. How is it, she muses, staring at the ripped froth of pink taffeta the princess shed by her black Italian riding boots with their gleaming silver buckles, that only two weeks ago, she and her husband, and Tatiana of course, had driven from Frankfurt to Normandy on terrifying motorways to spend Christmas in this château, and in that time the English woman was murdered? Now, it seems, everyday routines have become suspect. Even someone running a bath seems full of hidden meaning and malevolent intention.

The sky is a grey block, low on the flat land. A long drive leads up to the entrance of the château, and on the left, a small farm. The farmer's wife had laid a fire for the tourists before they arrived. In return they bought her a tin of shortbread from the ferry, taking it in turns to speak to her in a hybrid mash of languages, anxious to present themselves as amiable, likeable people. Somehow they understood each other. Who are they? her husband had asked her that evening. Friends of Pinar, she replied. How many of them are there this year? She had to think hard. Polish, Italian, German, North African, American, French. The farmer fondly watched his wife open the tin of shortbread with her neat small hands.

So the Inspector's wife is staying with us again?

His wife pretends to read the ingredients on the back of the tin.

I saw you washing the bed sheets. Enough blood to make people think we slaughter pigs.

Poor woman.

Her mouth is full of shortbread made with one hundred per cent butter. Yes, the château is busting with tourists this year. And their children.

The two young girls, Tatiana and Claudine, will dance with long ribbons, pink and blue, whirling them into dragons and silken flames while the adults look on. One of the girls will ask her father to hold her teddy bear in his arms and squeeze it so that Muzak oozes from the red plastic heart hidden in its paw. The English-man raises his glass. 'To simple things,' he says and they all lift their glasses, smiling as the heart in the bear's nylon paw lights up from the pulse of sound. Sprawled on a cushion next to the bear is a cat, a tiger cat from Paris, Biddy Ba Ba, who will stretch out in front of the fire and never go outside. He is agoraphobic and has to be picked up and put on the grass. Now Claudine puts down her ribbon, picks up the cat and runs outside in her ballet shoes to put him on the damp fern where he sits stricken and shivering in the rain. When she returns she starts to unpack her vanity case. Tatiana watches her friend carefully line six pairs of tiny ballet shoes on the window shelf. In the half-light of the fire they look like giant moths. Another toast. The American woman raises her glass. 'To new friends,' she suggests and everyone admires her daughter Claudine, who, red in the face, is doing the splits on the Persian rug.

'Between us all,' says Luciana's fat German husband, 'we are just about the entire European community.'

The oldest woman in the room interrupts him. 'Since when was I a European?'

'But you live in Europe, Yasmina?' Wilheim rubs his paunch, one eye on the English woman as she stretches her pale, freckled legs by the fire.

'So what?'

Claudine's mother laughs infectiously, all dimples and lustrous blue eyes. 'Nor me,' she declares. 'Je suis américaine.' They all look at the photographs on the wall, three of them, carefully placed underneath each other. The first is of the Spanish poet and playwright Lorca, in dinner jacket and tie, his face a perfect heart

6

shape. The second, a black and white photograph entitled 'Happy Memories of Avignon.' Three peasants, two men and a woman, sit around a wooden table eating bread and cheese under the heavy blossom of a chestnut tree. The third is a black and white photo of a rowing boat turned upside down on the River Lee in Hackney, London. 'I live near there.' The English woman points to the upturned boat. 'Hope they kept their mouths closed when the boat turned over.'

Luciana, her face covered in a mud pack which she will soon wash off with icy water, sings upstairs, odd lines like 'Sometimes it's hard to get my eyes to close.' She watches the mud mask crack with pleasure. Her husband, who sells real-estate in Frankfurt, does most of the cooking. 'There is nothing that makes him happier,' Luciana tells them all when she comes downstairs dressed for supper, 'than cooking for other people,' and they all peer at him through the glass doors of the kitchen as he rubs garlic into small squares of toast.

'Topless girls and cold beer, that's what makes me happy.' Philippe the French man smiles at his American wife. She can sip wine all night long without ever getting drunk. She smiles back at her dark Parisian husband of seven years, the father of her daughter. Her clothes are demure, but underneath her beige woollen skirt she wears stockings and black boned corsets that pull in her waist and make her hold her breath. Such a fair woman with such a dark man, and such an enchanted child, Claudine, who laughs deeply from the pit of her small stomach, dancing on her toes. Much-loved Claudine. Her heels never touch the floor.

The couple from England collect wood for the fire. Sometimes when they are alone in the damp forest he says to her, 'I love you, Mary,' and she replies, 'No, you don't. You just want something to love.' They throw the logs on to the fire and watch the flames hiss in silence. The two single women observe the couples with stony fascination. Yasmina, who keeps the greying curls off her face with two hairslides, is short and chainsmokes hand-rolled tobacco from a canary-yellow leather pouch. She was born in Sétif, Algiers. Clouds of tobacco smoke hide her face, as do the books she always carries with her, holding them close to her shortsighted eyes. Polish Monika, in her early thirties, glances clandestinely at the fifty-five-year-old Yasmina and wonders if she too will grow old alone, self-possessed and deceptively serene. Once the lover of a famous man who had a woman in every port, Monika has grown fat. Every night she sews by the fire, a brooding presence who for now has removed herself from all possible pain. The English man is drawn to her. When they all eat around the long table, his thin body leans in her direction, making sure she has enough of everything.

Tonight Philippe immaculately spoons fennel sauce on to everyone's fish, watched by Wilheim who, licking the garlic butter off his lips, wonders why he loathes the dark French man. A lamp in the shape of a globe of the world turns in the breeze from the window. At ten o'clock it moves from Arabia, the Arabian Sea, Sri Lanka and Colombo to Dondra Head.

The unloved watch the loved perform the small rituals of their loving.

At night they hear the cries of the loved from their solitary beds.

In the morning they watch the loved curiously.

They want rooms far away from their cries.

They want to be far away from the loved.

It hauls in their lovelessness too close.

But they also want to be near the loved.

Because the loved are blessed.

They want to be far away from the heat of the night, come together in the daytime for meals and light-hearted conversations because then they are more equal.

There are days when they do nothing but play music. The English man has an old 1930s accordion, the Algerian an oboe. Wilheim the German real-estate agent strums his guitar; the Parisian, light on his toes, plays the saxophone very badly, and his American wife sings – a glass of rosé in her hand. Luciana sings too, shrill operatic versions of whatever the American is singing, her voice strangely detached and harsh. The English woman looks into the fire, playing with her hair or the buckles on her shoes, listening and fidgeting. Sometimes she gets up and collects more wood, even though there is plenty. Monika, in her shapeless cardigans, peels an orange for Tatiana, bouncing her on her knee. She likes the girl and sometimes plays card games with her, talking in a mixture of German and English. Tatiana helps her repeat unfamiliar words, corrects her pronunciation and laughs when the Polish woman shouts 'Schnapps!' every time she wins a game.

There are baths and the cleaning of the bath. Shopping and the carrying of shopping back home. Meals and the preparation of meals, washing up and putting away. The keeping of the fire going, the sweeping of the floor, the washing down of the plastic tablecloth, the pouring of oil into the central-heating system, the rinsing of clothes, the reading of books, the changing into walking boots. The quiet times of people alone, thinking, sleeping, peeling apples, gutting fish. There is the watching of children's games and there is the playing of adult games. It is as if they have been marooned on an island, surrounded by the melancholy of frozen flat fields. Thin silver trees shiver in the wind. The postbox rusting next to the gate is always empty and the blue-green cedars that line the drive have no smell. This is the tamed wilderness that surrounds them, unlike the sea where all that is unknown lurks beneath the calm surface. There is, however, an escape route. A small road joins a bigger road that leads to the port. But no one wants to escape. The tourists play ping-pong in the attic upstairs, tournaments in combinations that are slightly flirtatious. Wilheim says to Mary every time she loses a game, 'Danke, danke schön.' The Algerian and the Parisian, swift, quick on their toes, score tricky points, watched by the American, whose perfume smells of milk and musk, the top of her stockings just visible as she lazily bends down to pick up an errant ball.

In this house, a tragedy occurred. The owners, a Spanish couple, sad at being childless for too long, adopted a baby girl from Mexico. They went to collect her when she was three weeks old and brought her back to Northern France. For six months the baby just lay on her back, black eyes staring at the ceiling. They thought it strange she was so still and silent but reckoned the long days of leaden sky and sleet in the winter months were a shock after the warmth of Mexico. When they discovered the baby girl they had searched so hard to find was brain-damaged, they hid all her picture books and tried to forget the plans they had made for her future. The baby seemed to watch them, never shutting her eyes, kicking her brown legs. One month later they paid for her to spend the rest of her life in a children's hospital in Paris, and then fled, distraught and guilty, back to Spain. So in the attic on the other side of the ping-pong table, something is covered in a brown blanket. A rocking horse with a real horse-hair mane, polished leather saddle and gleaming silver stirrups. In the small bedroom downstairs, white carved doves hang from nylon threads tied to the ceiling. A small wooden cot, like an empty coffin, stands beneath the birds. And now Pinar, the owner of the house, is pregnant – a miracle, she says to her husband, a miracle after being barren for so long, placing his hands on her huge belly so he can feel the child turn over. Sometimes she telephones the château, lying on her king-sized bed with its mosquito nets and pile of lavender pillows, concerned that everything is in order for her guests. Mary answers the phone and confesses shyly that she has forgotten her hostess's name.

'Pinar,' the English man whispers to her, and Mary says, 'It's Pinar, isn't it? Everything is fine here.'

2

Mary wades into the sea in her red woollen tights, hitching up her dress. She walks up to her ankles and then continues until the icy water laps around her waist and she can feel the weight of her clothes pulling her down. The English man, kneeling on the beach, shells in his lap, shouts out to her. She can feel the salt water touch her breasts through her thick cardigan. He shouts out to her again and the shells fall on to the sand. She has her back to him and hears his voice cracking against the wind. When the water touches her chin, she swims back to him fully clothed. A wave rushes over her head and he grabs at her wrists as she struggles to free herself, gasping from the many waves now pulling her back to sea. When he has dragged her twenty yards away from the white froth on the shore, she dips her hands into a puddle of water and wipes the salt off her face.

'That is a sewage pump.' They look at each other in silence and then he says, 'God placed two doors to hell by the gateway of a sewer. I don't know where I remember that from.' He picks up the shells that fell from his lap when he dragged her out of the sea.

'That's a fossil,' she says, disturbed to find she is weeping and cannot stop. They walk to a café. Every now and again she wrings out her clothes. He looks at her with fear in his eyes. 'I love you,' he says. 'No you don't,' she replies. 'You just wish you did.'

There are two questions he has not asked me, the weeping English woman thinks as she walks by his side. The first is, 'Why did you swim in the icy winter sea with all your clothes on?' He, the English man, is godfather to one of the little girls, Claudine. Every morning he makes her mushrooms on toast. She loves him. The morning he arrived, Claudine walked out into the grounds of the château and brought him one single mushroom she had picked, wrapped in a green leaf. She held it out to him while he laughed and kissed her and started to cook for her the many mushrooms he had bought at the market earlier on.

A little patch of eczema streaks across his left eyebrow. The second question he has not asked her is, 'Do you love me?' Perhaps he does not want to know. He never asks and she never explains.

They drink coffee in the deserted seaside café and she is shivering, watched curiously by the woman behind the counter. Mary shuts her eyes and the sound of the sea pounds through her head.

and the moon is green cheese
and the moon
and the moon
and the moon is green cheese

An eerie tin-man voice from inside a computer game breaks the silence. When they look up they see an acned heavy-metal fan playing with his toy, laughing at them from the next table.

'We are very English, aren't we? We love apples and roses from the garden. And muffins and honey. We like the rain. We like green pea soup and sofas and cardigans.' She shrugs, shivering and sad. 'I love you to my detriment.' His voice is suddenly throaty and harsh. 'You want to hurt everything that loves you. It's sick. It's boring. Go away. Don't come back.' He pays and they leave the café, running in the rain to the car. He drives and she shivers, all the time looking at the emerald eyes of the snake key-ring in the ignition.

'Do I know Pinar?' she asks him.

'Yes. She came to the house a couple of times.'

'Which house?'

'My house in London.'

'Did I meet her?'

'I think you did.'

'Why don't I remember her?'

'You forget things,' he says, putting his foot down. She finds herself thinking about the thirteen eggs the American woman bought in the market two weeks ago. They are beginning to smell.

3

The Inspector's cheeks are a little too flushed as he sips his fifth glass of burgundy. Luciana lethargically peels the shell off a pale prawn, one of many heaped on her plate.

'I am a meat man,' he says, patting his thickening stomach. Blanc has just eaten a large, bloody steak and is waiting for the waiter to bring the cheese.

'This is the land of seafood, cider, cheese and Calvados.' He waves his hand as if to capture the whole of Normandy. 'You have seen our orchards?' She nods and once again, as ever in her company, he can almost swear the strange blue of her eyes is unreal. Her gaze comes to him coloured by contact lenses, perhaps black, pressed over her pupils like small flying saucers.

'Yes, I have all this,' he says again as the cheese arrives and he cuts her a slice of creamy Camembert.

'But you speak as if you lack something, Inspector?' She leans forward to play with the cheese, chasing it across the plate before putting it into her mouth. He shrugs.

'The only thing I lack, Madame, is a solution to this case.

I want to close my files and take my vacation.' She nods, brushing the crumbs off her white shirt, which seems to be made from a web of fragile and revealing straps. A strange garment to wear in winter, he muses as he lights a cigar and changes the subject.

'The English man. Did he love her?'

'Oh yes. If anything it was she who was indifferent.'

He thinks this over, rolling the cigar between his finger and thumb, knowing that the Italian woman is watching his hands.

'Indifferent? Is that right? Was he angry with her, then?'

'Angry?'

'Of course. Wouldn't you be if your love was not reciprocated?'

'I am not interested.' She looks down at her plate and plays with the Camembert again.

'Angry,' he persists. 'Like your daughter.'

'Perhaps.'

'I have not asked you,' he risks, 'whether you work?'

'I am too rich to work.' She relaxes now. 'My husband is a good bank. He does not charge me interest.'

'He just gives you children.' The Inspector smiles at her.

'Yes.' She strokes her taut, flat stomach and seems to enjoy his curiosity. 'My husband and I like to holiday in Vienna. Wilheim enjoys the small pancakes and chocolate torte. There are no children to be seen in Vienna. That is what I enjoy.'

Blanc thinks about this for a while. 'But Goethe, Schumann and Kafka – they were children once?' She nods, and he notes that her face is devoid of expression marks. No wrinkles, no circles under her eyes, no furrows on her forehead.

'I look forward to the next generation,' she holds a prawn delicately between her fingers, 'because they will be robots.'

The burgundy has made him braver. 'You are a housewife?'

'There are days,' she says, 'when I stare into the carpet. We have a lot of carpet in our house in Frankfurt because it is very big. I imported it from Rome. It is blue, the blue of the Mediterranean.' She stops, as if to measure the effect of her words on the provincial Detective Inspector. 'There are days,' she repeats, 'when I do nothing but stare into the carpet. There are places, near the television set for example, where the blue deepens and I am sucked, abducted, into its dark centre. I am an alien in my own home, floating through the hyperspace of one hundred per cent wool.'

'You are daydreaming?'

'Of course.' She sips her Perrier. 'Unless you think I am mad?'

Blanc feels he has made a fool of himself. Who is she, this mocking Madame Bovary, staring all day at her carpets? This Italian suburban supermodel, catwalking the white surgical aisles of hypermarkets in Frankfurt. Clasping soap powder and pâté to her beautiful breasts as if they were Oscars.

'We were talking about the English man and his girlfriend. What makes you think he loved her?'

'He was attentive.'

Blanc smiles bitterly.

'All of us can imitate love, don't you agree?'

She runs her fingers through her hair and leans back in her chair, looking up at the crowded lunchtime restaurant.

'Love seems to be your speciality, Inspector?'

'Not at all,' he sighs.

'Are you married?'

The Inspector changes the subject. 'It is motive that I am after. It is not enough to feel love. More important is how we express love.'

He follows her gaze. It takes him to the first table by the door where a young, good-looking man with glossed slicked-back hair sits alone reading a newspaper. He has not taken off his heavy black and white checked winter overcoat despite the freakish heat of the wintery midday sun, and his bowl of soup is untouched.

'Can I give you a lift home, Madame?' He gestures to the waiter for the bill.

'No thank you. My husband will pick me up later.'

Blanc nods, takes a thick wad of bank notes out of his pocket and, without counting, throws the lot carelessly on to the white tablecloth.

'You are a generous man.' She smiles at him as he helps her put on her jacket, standing behind the divine woman as she slides her slender arms into the silk-lined sleeves. He notes that the man has put down his newspaper, lunch still untouched, and pays the bewildered waiter who is asking him if there is anything wrong with the food.

'Thank you for lunch, Inspector.' Luciana walks a little too fast for him. 'I hope I have been of some use to you.' He takes her hand and kisses her wrist. 'It was my pleasure,' he replies and, with a military nod of his head, walks painfully to his car.

'Were you ever in the army, Inspector?' she shouts after him.

'An officer in Algiers, Madame.' Fumbling for his indigestion pills, one hand on the wheel, the other searching in his jacket pocket, he thinks about the man she is waiting for. He is not going to sell the superfrau a carpet, that's for sure. Inspector Blanc radios a message to his colleague and leans his head against the window. An image of the lovely woman listening to Judy Garland in the splendour of her Frankfurt home, a circle of cucumber over each eye, presents itself to him. The brisk voice snarling from his radio startles him.

'Yes, we can see her, Inspector. She is talking to Professor Horse.'

'Is she now?' The Inspector feigns surprise. It is not like Horse to leave his food untouched. Nor is it characteristic of him to wear a heavy overcoat inside a restaurant. It looked more like a black and white checked blanket anyway. Perhaps the stallion is losing his highly tuned sense of style? Blanc always enjoys a canter with Horse. The next time they meet he resolves to fill his pockets with plenty of sugar lumps.

4

Tatiana brings her father five large cabbages from the garden.

'Look!' she shrieks, and father and daughter part the leaves to discover they are crawling with maggots. 'Never mind.' Wilheim squelches one of the slimy creatures between his fingers. 'No one will know. Get me the tomatoes from the fridge.' She does what she is told, holding her nose as she opens the fridge door. 'It stinks!' she shouts, just as the French man walks into the kitchen with a basketful of oysters. He looks at Tatiana with disgust as she pretends to vomit over her shiny new patent leather shoes. Wilheim glances at the thirteen eggs as yet untouched by anyone in the house and tells her to shut the fridge door. 'These are good.' Philippe expertly examines the oyster shells. 'I bought them in Dieppe this morning.' He watches Wilheim boil the leaves and the maggots alive, salvaging what is least bitten. 'The Germans like to turn the kitchen into a laboratory,' he says. Wilheim detects a small sneer on the French man's face. 'I suppose you are going to tell me I am a Nazi next?' He holds up a dead boiled maggot between his fingers. 'You see how small my hands are? My mother wanted me to be a surgeon.'

The oysters lie heaped on two silver platters, one at each end of the table. Nancy, her mousy blonde hair arranged in a neat plait, sits next to the English woman. She pours lemon juice on to her oyster and prods it with a little fork. 'Why don't you eat any?' she asks Mary.

'Because I don't like them.'

'Ah.' The American slides it down her throat. 'Try one. Look, you prod here, and if they are fresh they move.'

'No thanks.'

The American eats another and her eyes shine. 'You know, eating oysters is like oral sex.' Lemon juice runs down her chin.

'Oh,' the English woman replies, watching the oyster shrink from the steel prong of the fork. Everyone applauds when Wilheim brings the stuffed cabbage to the table.

In the next room Claudine and Tatiana are dissecting a plastic monster in the dark. They split the middle of its belly and slide their hands inside. Green slime glows on their fingers as they remove the organs from the centre of the beast. Tatiana whispers and points, 'That is the brain, that is the heart, that is the liver and those are the ovaries so it must be a woman.'

Monika pokes her finger through one of the holes in the cabbage leaf. 'To be in love is to be bitten,' she suggests in her hard, sarcastic voice. By candlelight the amber heart she wears on a chain around her neck looks like a cancerous birth mark. Jilted lover. Betrayed, grown fat, she sleeps in the coldest room in the house under a pile of heavy blankets. 'Claudine, come and eat!' the American shouts to her daughter. Tonight she wears a blue velvet dress making her blue eyes more lustrous than ever. 'Non. Non. Non,' Claudine shouts and her father shrugs. 'Leave her.' Luciana wipes her lips with a napkin. She wears a tiger's eye ring on her long finger and pours more rosé into Monika's glass. 'That rosé is industrial,' Philippe says, looking at the label on the bottle. 'Never mind.' Luciana smiles at him. 'Monika likes it.' Monika tucks a greasy curl behind her ear. 'You have a child in Poland?' The Polish woman nods, devouring her cabbage.

The American raises her finely plucked eyebrows.

'Really? Is that so?'

'Perhaps,' the English woman suggests to the American, who has just lit a Camel Light and stares curiously at the Polish woman. 'Perhaps she does not want to talk about it.' Something glitters in Luciana's golden hair. An invisible silken web, a kind of hairnet studded with small rhinestones. Now she spoons some cream on to the Polish woman's lemon tart. 'I don't mind talking,' Monika shrugs as Tatiana runs into the room, her hands covered in green slime.

'If you have just finished heart surgery,' Luciana reprimands her daughter, 'you should wash your hands before you eat.'

Wilheim ruffles the girl's hair. 'It is not normal for children to be clean all the time.' Tatiana climbs into Monika's lap and bursts into tears. 'Don't cry, we're having a party.' Monika wipes the slime off the girl's hands with her napkin and feeds her spoonfuls of lemon tart. Luciana brushes imaginary crumbs off her black linen lap.

'In Gdansk,' Monika begins, 'I worked in the shipyard. Every day I had to climb into a huge cylinder, very dark and deep, and clean it. There were steel stairs to climb down and up again, but it was still very dark and sometimes my lamp would go out. I was not happy but this is normal. It is normal to be unhappy.'

Wilheim pours the coffee while Luciana spoons sugar into Monika's cup. 'Three, four?' She smiles at the Polish woman who, charmed, nods even when Luciana opens her weird eyes wide and whispers, 'Six, seven, perhaps eight sugars, Monika?' The English woman interrupts. 'It is not normal to be unhappy,' she insists, watching Ben disappear into the kitchen. 'Chocolate biscuits,' he says cheerily when he returns, holding up the packet. Only Tatiana takes one.

'Stick your biscuits up your arse.' The English woman throws her napkin down and leaves the table.

'She's gone to look at the rocking horse.' Tatiana gleefully sucks the chocolate off her biscuit.

'Exciting.' Monika is a little drunk.

'I told you I cleaned the cylinders in the shipyard?' Everyone nods, including Claudine who has now crept into the room, the ribbons of her ballet shoes trailing on the floor. 'One morning I put on my overalls and climbed down there with my bucket and brush. I cleaned for about ten minutes and then my lamp went out. It was pitch black and I could not see anything. Someone grabbed hold of me. I screamed but of course no one can hear, it is very deep there, maybe thirty foot. This person held my arms behind my back. When he pulled up my dress and overalls I knew it was a man. He raped me.'

Tatiana reaches for another biscuit. 'So I became pregnant,' Monika says in a matter-of-fact voice. 'My grandmother said I must go and tell the manager of the shipyard what had happened. She came with me and there was a big meeting. It was decided that because none of the workers would own up, the whole shipyard was to be the child's father. Every man who worked there had to pay out of his wages towards clothes and food for the rest of its life. My child is called the Gdansk Baby because she has thousands of fathers.'

Luciana yawns, adjusting her invisible hairnet. A galaxy of turquoise rhinestones shimmers above her golden head.

'Goodnight!' She waves her hand vaguely in the direction of the dinner table and walks out of the room. Tatiana plays with the amber heart that rests malevolently between the Polish woman's large breasts.

'Do you like your baby?' she whispers.

'No. I do not like her. I did not choose to have a child.'

The American, who smells of velvet and vanilla candy, turns to Yasmina, suddenly morose. 'You must tell me more about my mother.' Her blue eyes fill with drunken tears that trickle prettily down her cheek.

'Do you know Nancy's mother?' The English man scratches his elbow and then immediately takes his hands away from the rash creeping into his arm. Philippe feels sorry for him. What is wrong with the maudlin English woman? Scorning his oysters and then humiliating her boyfriend in front of them all.

'Chérie, don't cry.' He puts an arm protectively around his wife. The Algerian woman points to the globe. 'When it turns to North Africa I will tell you about your mother,' she promises, thinking that it is not his wife the French man needs to protect from his own anger but the sullen English woman.

Everyone goes to bed except Wilheim. He takes his brandy and sits near the fire thinking about the three large condominiums that are to be built next year in California. He has to arrange for twelve Elite models to be flown to L.A. so he can be photographed with them. They will wear the briefest of bikinis and he will wear a suit. The eternal fat old kraut, he muses, perspiring and bald, grinning pathetically in the middle of this bouquet of whore princess flesh. Despising him and not one of them over twenty.

When Mary comes downstairs to get a glass of water, his slate-grey eyes take in her shabby blue dressing-gown and mousy hair flattened from sleep. 'I am restructuring my debts,' he says. She looks pale and vacant. He pours her a brandy, gesturing for her to sit with him by the fire. She is thin, he thinks, and probably bruises easily, that bony English type with freckles on her back. She drinks her brandy in one go, hunched into herself. He fills her glass again and lets his thoughts wander to the bar he could buy in a mall near the condominium. He would theme it, glamorise it, name it after those old Hollywood movies where men wore hats and women wore gloves and both of them wanted each other, dancing cheek to cheek in rooms full of potted palms. The globe moves across Hubli, Madras and Patna.

'You were right, what you said at dinner,' he says. 'It is not normal to be unhappy.' She looks bemused but when she speaks her voice is calm and detached.

'What do you think the East and West Germans can teach each other?'

He laughs at her question, strangely aroused.

'They can't teach me anything. I don't want to learn how to be a soldier or how to drive a Trabant. They have to learn our ways. They think they are always right. It's not going to be easy for them.' The well-fed German watches her scratch her mosquito bites. 'You are an interesting woman,' he says. 'You are very private and very open at the same time.' Unsettled by her silence, he continues.

'The angrier you are the more the mosquitoes move in. That is because when you are angry your blood boils.' Her distracted eyes settle on his fat tan face and then she stares at a calendar on the wall instead. Wilheim is curious. She knows I am staring at her but she doesn't care. This interests him. Eventually he says, 'One morning I was walking in the mountains and a woman naked from the waist rode towards me on a horse. She stopped and said hello, her voice very deep. And then she rode away again. As I walked on, I saw a pair of women's pants, hanging from a bush of thorns. It was erotic because it frightened me.'

The English woman nods.

'Luciana,' he says, 'should make an exercise video. It would give her something to do and give her a private income. But she does not like exercise so that is no good.' He wonders if she is naked under her dressing-gown.

'What do you want to do with your life, Mary?'

'I want to die.'

'What for?'

'My country.' To his surprise, she guffaws.

'Perhaps you think life is not interesting?' He pours himself more brandy. 'It is only electricity that is interesting.' The ring on his finger, a thick band of gold, glitters by the light of the fire. 'Ideas, money, the promise of sex, expression, taste, opinion,' he spits the words out. 'That is interesting.'

She shrugs.

'The English are accomplished degenerates.' Wilheim runs his fat finger over his teeth.

'Only aristocrats,' she says, and seems startled to hear her own voice.

The fat man sighs. 'Love is not interesting. It is hard work. Love is anguish.'

'I'd like a kebab right now,' she interrupts in her flat, guileless voice.

'If I were to dress you,' he brings his chair closer to hers, 'you would be barefoot and I would shave off your hair.'

'Why?'

'So you would look like the victim you feel.' He takes a sip of his brandy.

When Wilheim sticks his tongue into Mary's mouth she digs her nails into the back of his hands. And when he strokes her breasts under her dressing-gown with his swollen fingers, she pinches the folds of pink flesh at the back of his neck. Encouraged, he unbuttons her shabby dressing-gown and licks her stomach. She bites his shoulder through the navy cotton of his shirt. Real bites. Like he is meat. She wants him to hurt and bleed. She is repulsed by him and she wants him, electrifying her.

'You are married,' she whispers stupidly and the German pulls away from her, tugging at the band of gold on his finger.

'Marriage?' He points to the red welt where the ring was, running the cold metal down her stomach towards her thin pale thighs.

'Papa.'

Tatiana peers at her father through the half-open door, trailing a blanket in her unwashed hand. She slowly walks to him, taking agonising fairy steps, journeying to her father across an infinity of carpet. He waits for her patiently and she lets him wait, taking her time until at last she asks him to kiss her goodnight, which he does, his lips wet from the kiss before.

'Take me to bed,' she commands in a mock-sleepy voice. Her father strokes her tangled hair, whispering comforting things to her as he picks her up in his arms, engrossed with her, adoring her, and carries her out of the room, a proud groom and his yawning girl bride.

Mary, abandoned, does up the buttons of her childish blue dressing-gown and stares at the pile of white ashes where the fire once was.

5

There is an unspoken conspiracy of silence about the thirteen rotting eggs in the fridge. Even the children no longer joke about the smell in the kitchen. Everyone opens the fridge to get cheese or ham or milk and holds their breath. Outside, Biddy Ba Ba's stomach drags against the gravel on the drive as he cries out in terrible secret pain at the odourless cedars and mud fields beyond.

When the telephone rings and Philippe runs towards it, the English man stops him. 'I'll take this call.' The French man notices the authority in his voice and, in contrast, the violent skin disease on the back of his hands. 'Marat,' he jokes, but Ben has already turned his back on him.

'Pinar?'

'The baby is growing too quickly,' Pinar moans. 'My belly is huge, I can hardly walk. I'm listening to Mozart. What sort of person will my child turn out to be? I can hear Tatiana and Claudine playing near you . . . let me listen . . . where are they?'

'In the TV room.'

have you seen the red girl – clap clap
in her red skirt – clap clap
tomorrow she will go to the priest – clap clap
wakes up with a baby – clap clap
he doesn't want to eat – clap clap clap clap

'How is everything? My breasts hurt. I sleep on my side now. We are so happy. This is what I have prayed for. Lit candles in church for. Do you mind me talking all the time?'

'No.'

'I eat ice-cream every day for the calcium. It's due any day now. I'm tired all the time. My skin is good but I'm afraid of my hair falling out. What if there's something wrong with the child? But they've done all the scans and it all seems okay. Is the central heating working?'

'Everything is perfect.'

'Do you play music, all of you?'

'Yes, we play every day.'

'I wish I could be with you. I eat too much meat and can't have enough avocados. Do you think it will harm the child to drink a little red wine?'

'No.'

'Are you using the dishwasher?'

The English man suddenly drops the telephone and cries out. A large white rat scuttles over his shoes and runs across the room.

'Ben, where are you? What's happening?'

The rat's thick tail thuds against the floor in a panic. The English man picks up an empty wine bottle and tiptoes towards it.

'Where are you? What's happening, Ben? Is something wrong?'

Biddy Ba Ba sits tangled in the satin ribbons of Claudine's ballet shoes, growling as the English man moves a chair and takes a swipe at the rat. When he knocks it against the wall, a yellow frothy liquid spills from its mouth and the English man smashes the bottle over its head. The glass breaks. Ben and Philippe, shocked, watch the white beast throw its bloody body at the wall, refusing to die. Ben picks up another bottle and hits out with all his strength one last time. It shudders and yelps, a high-pitched desperate cry. This time the English man cracks its skull beneath his boot.

'Pinar? It's okay. It was just a rat. I'll call you later.'

He puts the telephone down and he is shaking. They stare at the blood and fur. 'I had a dream of death.' The English man is short of breath. 'I saw a blue tunnel of light, very dark blue in the centre. It was not frightening. It came towards me but it was not frightening.'

Philippe starts to clear up the rat.

'I dreamt she was tearing my hair out like leaves,' Ben says.

The French man is crouched down by the rat, trying to wrap it in newspaper. 'Who was tearing out your hair?'

'Mary.'

'It is so big.' Philippe shakes his head. The corpse's feet hang over the sides of the newspaper.

'I want to make love to her but she won't let me.' The English man scratches his cheek.

'Is she a cold woman?' Philippe puts the bloody bundle into the dustbin, but it won't quite fit. Its tail sticks macabrely out of the garbage and the two men have to push it down, groaning and shaking their heads.

'When I touch her she stiffens until I let go.'

They prepare a bowl of soapy water to clean up the blood on the skirting-board.

'Why don't you kill her?' Philippe leans against the wall and lights a cigarette.

'I would like to sometimes.' Ben stares at the pool of vomit the rat threw out of its mouth.

'But who knows? We might grow old together and drink Darjeeling in the garden.'

> *what's the meaning of life – clap clap*
> *asked the butcher's big fat wife – clap*
> *a round of white and a fat pork slice – clap clap*
> *chops and steak and roast lamb twice – clap clap clap*

Claudine and Tatiana lie on their stomachs in the TV room. Tatiana is reading to Claudine from the faded yellow pages of an old exercise book, all the while keeping a nervous eye on the door.

'It's all right,' the younger girl whispers. 'They're killing the rat.'

Tatiana squints at the page. 'Who is she?'

'My grandmother.' Claudine reaches for the book.

Tatiana possessively moves the battered diary away from the grasping fingers of the princess girl. Today it is her turn to wear the paper crown and she wears it with pride on her gleaming yellow hair. Tatiana wants to keep the diary for ever and read it at her own leisure and in absolute privacy. Like Claudine, she knows this book is forbidden to her. The thought sends small electric shocks through her fingers as she turns the pages.

'Tangier 1956. I say: Hey Jim, just want to connect you up to a few things. I don't trust you. I don't respect you. I guess we should split. He says, Jane, you've been so moody these past six weeks, I don't think I want to live with you. Right now, Jim, I feel like I can't sit in the same room as you, never mind share a pillow. When you don't feel it in your body, well, you don't feel it.'

Claudine also wants the diary for her own. Despite her fear at being caught stealing her mother's possessions, she plays greedily with the letters and labels that fall from between the pages: an old postcard of a group of women in red headdresses adorned with silver and amber jewels, men in blue robes sitting on white mehari camels, advertisements for Texaco gasoline, faded cards with the telephone numbers of embassies, airports, hospitals and *gendarmeries* printed in bold colours. Claudine holds on tight to her stolen booty; while Tatiana reads in a low whisper, she moves closer so their heads touch.

'Tangier 1956. Jim says: Nothing in the world can hurt me as much as you. Suicide is rage, Jane.

'Thing is, if you want to die you want to die. I don't see the point of being brave and pretending to look forward to the future.

Not all of us want to work at not being sad. Not all of us want to wring life for every experience it will give us. Some of us don't want to be conscious anymore. Consciousness is a curse. Listen, some of us are too clever to pretend to raise our pathetic glasses of champagne to a long life and universal joy and all that shit. Some of us don't want to accumulate knowledge and understanding in the hope that what is called the human spirit will make it all worthwhile. Some of us are just not up to all the things that being alive brings to your doorstep. Why should I pretend that they are part of complexity and make life interesting? No. I don't want another long sad day.'

Tatiana cups her hand over Claudine's ear. 'She shot herself.'

'I knew she was going to.'

The older girl makes her voice sound blasé and bored. 'This next bit is only about a cat.'

'Read it to me,' Claudine commands. 'She's my grandmother.'

'Oh boy! We got a new kitten. But Jim gives her chicken bones and I get scared for it. We had a kitten that once choked to death on chicken bones. Jim works all day but he can't pay the rent with physics. Every equation he works on ends in zero anyhow. He doesn't care. Sometimes I think I should work out who owes me what for the odd article and story and move out with the kids. But hell's bells. What a waste of the little we've made together and all we've been through. A waste of all the fights and tears and making up. Sometimes I just can't believe I'm a mother. I feel more like Marilyn – y'know, all tits and lips – biting her diamond earrings. Eating diamonds for the camera! It is not that thought that makes me think I'm her. It's her lonesome eyes. Yeah. I'm always on painkillers like her, eating happy pills and smiling sweet. One day a sheriff and his dep will have to search the outback for me.'

'If your father comes in pretend to be asleep,' Tatiana whispers, strangely excited by the violent way her friend chews her lips as she listens to her grandmother's morbid words.

'Tangier 1957. I got a new nail varnish: tremendous pearl lustre to lift the heart. Also a new yellow silk blouse, the colour of lemons. Guess I want someone to squeeze me hard! Husband Jim and Wife Jane, that's me, talked last night about the possibility of separation. This has resulted in some queasiness on both our parts. We look at each other in a new cruel way; cool and judgmental when we used to have a warm eye. Leonora is staying with us for a while. I washed her long red hair for her this morning and we talked – the hours flew by and I was happy. I'd forgotten what that feels like. As ever, I'm always mighty cheered by thinking people – whatever meaning they've made for themselves.

'What a catalogue of snot, tears and misery. Let me change the tone and lighten things up. I like the small wooden desk I write on. I like my blue sleeveless summer dress and silver pots of mint tea. I like hammering the keys of the typewriter and then stopping for a long time, running my hands over the soft blonde hair on my shins, listening out for Nancy and Sam, little sweethearts, all cosied up in their bunkbeds for a siesta. I like Jim kissing me at the end of the day and us drinking beer and cooking supper together, and I like walking hand in hand through the souks. And I like the unfiltered cigarettes I smoke too many of. Yesterday I cut up a cigarette pack into ten little squares, and I wrote my name and address on every one of them, and I couldn't figure out why. Now I know. Should something happen to me, I want people to know where my kids are. I want them to look after Sam and Nancy while the cleaning-woman mops up my guts from the blue and white tiles in the kitchen.'

'Give me the book.' Claudine nudges Tatiana's arm in a panic as she hears her father making his way to the TV room. When Philippe opens the door, he finds the two girls in a deep sleep, curled on their sides, the TV flickering over their bare arms and shins. He walks over to his daughter and kisses her forehead, comforted by her presence after the bloody spectacle of the rat. When he strokes her hair, careful not to knock off the paper princess crown, the girl holds her breath, counting to twenty until her father, at last, tiptoes out of the room. 'I just want codeine and a margarita,' Tatiana drawls in a ruined broken whisper, stabbing a biro into her heart as she watches Claudine creep out of the room with the diary tucked under the white cotton of her dress. She knows exactly what the princess with her tiny feet is going to do. She is going to run up the stairs and slide the diary under her mother's underwear at the bottom of the black suitcase.

'Did you ever read my mother's stories?' Nancy asks the Algerian as they watch the women of Rouen, in their high heels and golden crucifixes, trail little dogs on leads around the square. 'She wrote

one where a woman cooks her husband's dog after an argument.'
The American throws back her head and laughs. 'I'm glad Claudine has boring parents like me and Philippe.' Both women are
shopping for sea perch because guests of Monika's are coming
to supper. When Philippe asked the Polish woman if she wanted
him to make a lemon sauce for the fish, she said, 'They can
eat shit.'

A potbellied performer in purple shorts, his long black hair tied
back in a pony-tail, lies on a bed of nails, watched by a circle of
children. He drinks a gallon of paraffin, torches his lips and blows
out flames into the crowd. The American woman shouts out to
him to light her cigarette and everyone laughs. They are sitting
on a bench with bags of shopping on their laps. When Nancy
smokes, she looks like an old-style hostess at a dinner party, lively
and alert, effortless easy company. She could be wearing a
thin-strapped cocktail dress, glass of champagne held laconically
in one hand, cigarette in the other, a Mississippi belle who made
it to the metropolis to browse in bookshops and sip lazy coffees
in cafés. She flicks through the copy of *Le Monde* on her lap,
smoking and looking down the columns for gossip. 'When I met
Philippe he said come and live with me and I will build you a
bathroom. It was a clever thing to say because as a child in Tangier we had no bathroom. After Mom died, Dad just got on with
his science research while we took showers in the shed outside.
Our fridge was run from a gas bottle and if we had to go in
the night we'd all pee into a red bucket we kept in the
bedroom.'

A huddle of children run into the circle to put money into the performer's basket. When the little girls kiss his cheek he roars, 'Merci, merci, chérie,' and they run away as fast as they can, scared and giggling.

'The first time Philippe and I slept together I was wearing a very smart suit, you know, a short skirt and jacket a friend had lent to me. It was black, kind of like a sexy widow, and I wore it with a pair of red high-heeled shoes. As we were going up the stairs to his apartment, Philippe said, "You are the wife I have dreamt about. She wears a suit like the one you are wearing." I thought, Gee, but this isn't even mine. Perhaps I should give him my friend's telephone number! He had an order for things. First we had to drink pastis. Then we had to eat the chicken he had cooked and finish a bottle of wine. And then after he had blown out the candles on the table and cleared the plates we had to make love. "You are too structured for me," I said. "You would want me to put spoons in the drawer in a certain way." "That is what you must bring to me," he insisted. "You must bring to me your way of doing things." '

The man stands up from his bed of nails and roars again. Waving a caveman club he walks out into the crowd, bashing them over the heads until they reach into their pockets and give him more money. He prises a woman away from her partner and orders her to oil his pregnant tattooed stomach. When he gives her a dart and tells her to aim just above his belly button, she refuses, shaking her head with horror. 'Please, please,' he cajoles her. She shakes her head and grimaces. The caveman roars and threatens to cull her with the club until she reluctantly takes aim and the dart falls off his great greased belly. 'Kisses hurt more!' he shouts to the crowd.

'My father didn't care if we lived on sour milk for a week before the next cheque came in. His work was everything. An interesting life was everything. But Philippe does not just care about himself. First thing for him is to feed his wife and child. You know what I love most about Philippe? He's never worn a denim jacket covered in funky patches from San Francisco. He always looks smart. After Dad and what happened to Mom in Tangier, all that dope and expatriate life, it's kind of cool to have a guy who looks like any other when you walk down the road.'

Nancy opens a bag of nuts coated in sugar. After a while she says, 'Tell me about my mother, Yasmina.' The Algerian woman shakes her head. 'It will take too long.' Nancy's lustrous blue eyes fill instantly. 'When you are five years old it is very difficult to believe your mother is dead. She made me little mice out of radishes, you know, when she wasn't writing.'

Yasmina says, 'My mother died when I was five too.'

Nancy's mouth is full of sugared nuts. 'I'm sorry.'

Yasmina stares at the American.

'How is it,' she asks, 'that you never ask me about myself?'

The American blushes. 'I want to,' she replies quickly.

'How do you think I live?'

'Huh?'

'Some of us don't have husbands and children.'

'Yeah, well, you teach. Don't you?'

'Yes.'

'See, I do know. You teach history at a university in London.'

'So,' Yasmina assumes a tone of voice that is familiar to them both. 'What do we already know about you?'

'My mother's name was Jane, my father's name was Jim.'

'Yes.'

'Like a lot of beatnik Americans, they lived for a while in Tangier.'

'Yes.'

'My mother shot herself.'

'Yes.'

Nancy never asks, 'Why did my mother shoot herself?' Instead, the American changes the mood. 'Let's go and have a beer.'

'I don't drink.' Yasmina smiles. 'You see, you know nothing about me.'

When Nancy does not reply, she says, 'Who are these friends of Monika's, then?'

'The man she loved and his girlfriend.' Nancy watches Yasmina walk towards the tattooed man, jingling coins in her hand. She drops them into the hat near his bed of nails.

They pick up their shopping and walk to the Hôtel-Dieu hospital where the eleven-year-old Flaubert, son of the chief surgeon, ran with his sister through the hospital wards.

Peering through the windows of the autopsy laboratory, the two women stare at a child-birth demonstrator, a giant female rag doll that lies in a heap on the marble slab. The American woman does not want the Algerian to spill out the entire contents of her foreign head. She wants to fast-forward the narrative from her point of view and stop at a few selected scenes. But she is at the mercy of the stubborn story-teller, who seems to have declared a secret 'all or nothing' ultimatum. Nancy secretly knows and dreads that Yasmina will ruin her version of history for ever. Story-tellers, she muses, are just evangelists with dandruff on their shoulders. They should get drunk, tell a few anecdotes and then fall over.

'This is Gustav.' Monika's Polish face is powdered into a paler version of herself. She looks like a Noh mask: black kohl eyes and lips the colour of a recent massacre. She has painted an expression that will hide her own, and presents herself to the assembled company as the star player in a drama they have been invited to participate in – though they do not know the story. These unwitting players will have to make up their lines as they go along.

Monika looks happy. Gustav holds her in his arms for slightly too long and then shakes hands with Philippe, Ben and Wilheim. For the women, the bit parts in this scenario, he smiles and nods in a warm and chivalrous manner. He rolls their names across his tongue, 'Luciana, Yasmina, Nancy, Mary,' giving each a smoky inflection. 'And this is Sylvia,' Gustav gestures to the awkward bleached-blonde eighteen-year-old standing at his side, a ruched leather jacket draped over her shoulder. 'Sylvia,' Monika announces, 'is an astrologer.' Everyone understands the plot. Sylvia will play the girlfriend, Monika will play the wronged lover, and Gustav the guilty philanderer. Nancy says, 'I don't want to know about the future. If I thought about my life everything would close down.'

MONIKA: This is Gustav. [*They embrace.*]

GUSTAV: And this is Sylvia.

MONIKA: Sylvia is an astrologer.

NANCY: I don't want to know about the future. If I thought about my life everything would close down.

'We've bought two apple tarts.' Sylvia points to the white box on the table tied with yellow ribbon. Monika's powdered face leans to the left in a thank-you gesture as she glides across the room towards a tray of wine glasses. 'The future is always melancholy because it is there our dreams are supposed to become reality,' Sylvia suggests to Nancy.

Monika interrupts.

'The porcelain teapot just near your elbow, Gustav.' Gustav removes his elbow, which is precariously near the sixteenth-century teapot, just in time. 'Look.' He waves his cigarette in the direction of the barn. Everyone murmurs at the sight of a hawk, hovering above the roof.

MONIKA: This is Gustav. [*They embrace.*]

GUSTAV: And this is Sylvia.

MONIKA: Sylvia is an astrologer.

NANCY: I don't want to know about the future. If I thought about my life everything would close down.

SYLVIA: We've bought two apple tarts. [*Monika distributes wine.*]

SYLVIA: [*To Nancy*] The future is always melancholy because it is there our dreams are supposed to become reality.

MONIKA: The porcelain teapot! Just by your elbow, Gustav.
GUSTAV: Look! [*They all look at a hawk circling the barn outside.*]

Monika needs another language. She is badly, fatally hurt. The apocalyptic, the inflammatory, the controversial and contradictory – Monika cannot afford them this evening. There is no love without rage, that is why the script is ridiculous. Love and Rage, the four-letter furnace that will torch the stage sofa and consume them all. Monika wants to destroy Gustav. Gustav, to survive Monika's rage, has to have not nine but infinite lives. In the room next door, Tatiana and Claudine watch Terminator on the TV reassemble himself after multiple woundings.

'I so much want,' Gustav slides a forkful of sea perch into his mouth, 'for the young people of Poland to try out something of their own.' He looks across the table and finds Monika's eyes. 'Some things are worth suffering for.'

'Like what?' Monika watches Gustav smear a thick layer of butter on to his bread roll.

'Freedom.'

'Oh,' she says.

'I am sad particularly for the dead of Romania who did not live to see the future they shed blood for.'

Wilheim looks across the table and finds Mary's eyes. He says, 'Now that socialism is dead, we have to live more experimentally.'

'Socialism is not dead,' Mary replies. 'As long as people are not equal, socialism is not dead.'

'We are all unequal all of the time,' Monika interrupts. 'Isn't that right, Sylvia?'

Sylvia tucks her blonde hair behind her ears. 'Enjoy the present and let the future take care of itself!'

'Sylvia's surname is Starr,' Monika explains to Luciana.

Gustav puts his hand protectively on Sylvia's thigh.

Monika wants to suck this sad night out of herself for ever.

Gustav and Monika walk in the dark towards the barn. 'I would really like to know.' He pauses, and she holds her breath. What is it the man she loves, but who no longer loves her, wants to know? That she wants to stab a screwdriver into his eyes? 'I would like to know what the recent events in Eastern Europe mean to you.' She is ashamed of how much pain she is in at this moment. The amber heart she wears around her neck feels like a teenager's trinket. 'They mean we must seriously listen to people who are unhappy,' she says. When they come to the end of the path they stand uncomfortably by the barn door, looking out at the cedars. 'Communism was the last dream.' His voice is sad and flirtatious. 'Monika, do you think there is no past and no future, just capitalism?' She bends down in the dark, and gathers something up into her arms. Biddy Ba Ba cries into her breast.

'There is only revenge.'

The English man looks at his watch, puzzled. 'It's almost stopped.' Mary peers at his wrist. When she sees the violent red streaks of his rash, she takes some ice from her water and gently rubs it on the back of his hand. 'It's slowed right down,' she says. 'The hands are flickering.' Philippe looks over Ben's shoulder. 'Like that rat,' he jokes. 'Your watch is in its last death throes, like the feet of the rat.'

'What rat?' Nancy looks at the other women, confused.

'You were out enjoying yourself.' Philippe refills their glasses. 'Apart from Mary. She never enjoys herself.' Everyone smiles at Mary. She shrugs, wringing her hands as she continues her conversation with Monika who has just returned from her walk. Everyone wants to know about the rat, but Gustav stops them in a mock-commanding voice. 'Line up for a photo before I go. I bought a new camera today.' Luciana runs upstairs to get the lipstick all the women admire and demand they wear for the photo call. 'It is called Indian Mysore,' the Italian says wryly when she returns. 'It looks different on everyone.'

'I am partial to lipstick.' Gustav points his lens at her and clicks.

'I was not ready.' Luciana's voice is steely as she pulls her cashmere cardigan from the back of a chair and puts it on.

The image is instant. It whirs out of the camera and they all watch it develop in silence.

'Here.' He gives the photograph to the perfect flawless woman without looking at it, by way of apology. When everyone gathers around Luciana to admire it, Gustav clicks again.

The unloved look brave.

The unloved look heavier than the loved. Their eyes are sadder but their thoughts are clearer. They are not concerned with pleasing or affirming their loved one's point of view.

The unloved look preoccupied.

The unloved look impatient.

Gustav and Sylvia walk to the car hand in hand, man and girl, he beeping his horn, she waving, waving and blowing kisses to Biddy Ba Ba who makes little noises in his throat as he watches them from the window.

6

'Chéri chéri chéri chéri chéri chéri chéri chéri,' the American woman moans from the room next door.

'Say you respect me,' she cries out. 'Say it say it say it say it!'

They scream and then they murmur, the springs of the bed wheezing and she crying out long and loud while he whispers something and her voice, angry and desperate, replies, 'Say you goddamn respect me.'

Monika lies alone under her pile of heavy blankets, naming every cake she wants to eat. Gugelhopf, Käsekuchen, Sachertorte, Apfelstrudel. She is thinking about the conversation she could have had with Gustav. When she was visiting friends in Moscow, she, like everyone else, waited in a queue that snaked around three blocks to taste a delicious piece of the West in the new McDonald's. A double cheeseburger cost the equivalent of two hours' pay: McDonald, the benovolent father feeding hamburgers to fifteen thousand people a day. Around the corner, embalmed in his tomb, Lenin the father who put black bread on the table – but not every day. Actors dressed as cartoon characters amused the people waiting in line, watched by a statue of Alexander Pushkin. An eighty-year-old disabled war veteran limped to the front of the line and showed his ID card which gave him priority in queues. When he was served his Big Mac he sat down, stared at it for half an hour, and then eventually ate it with a spoon. He told Monika how he had come from Sverdlovsk to Moscow for medical treatment, but at Pushkin Square saw the crowd and joined in. It was longer than the queue for Lenin's tomb of course. In between mouthfuls he told her that in his view the communists in his country had been very cruel to their people. This did not mean that communism was bad, only that some people were cruel. She could not tell this to Gustav because he had been very cruel to her. She would not be interested in what he had to say because she would identify him with cruel régimes. He had offered her a future and betrayed her.

How is it she can name cakes but not bridges built over great dams and estuaries? Why is it she is not thinking about the future of Poland but she is thinking about a Polish man who said, 'A man does not love a woman if he cannot beat her'? Why is it she does not spend her days reading great works of art, but instead idles away the hours thinking about a new perfume she feels will change her life? There are fictions, technologies, geographies, and there is poetry. There is coherence, incoherence and exhilaration. There is attraction and playing it cool and there is attraction and abandon. There is love and there is ambivalence, but there is mostly ambivalence. And there is freedom. What do you do with freedom? This is a conversation she could have had with Gustav.

There are so many conversations she could have had with Gustav. Instead she has them with herself. There is her grandmother in Warsaw, too shy to ask overseas visitors to bring toilet paper, and there is her uncle in America who calls the toilet the bathroom. And there is her child. Monika begins naming cakes again.

Mary tiptoes into the bedroom, her bare feet cold on the floorboards. She takes off her clothes.

'Look,' she says, and naked, turns a cartwheel.

'That's very good.' The English man peers over the blankets. 'Do it again.'

She lifts her hands above her head and turns two more perfect cartwheels.

'Very good,' he says again. 'Do something else.'

She does a handstand.

'Hmmmm,' he says.

She gets into bed. 'You are a very lucky man.'

'Why?'

'Only Swedish au pairs are supposed to do things like that.'

'Oh,' he says, smiling.

'Stroke me,' she whispers, breathless from the cartwheels.

Ben's raw red hands press into her stomach, and then slide down her thighs.

'I love you,' she says.

The English man reaches over and switches off the light.

Sleepless and lustless in her electronic nightworld, Luciana stares into the infinity of her computer screen. One hand on her sharp hip, the other on the keyboard, she disrobes an image of herself: a virgin Luciana whose innocence waits for a conqueror. She strokes her techno breasts and watches her virtual ribcage expand as her breathing heightens. Luciana reinvents herself over and over again on a piece of software. Now she wears a choker made from crab claws; a chain of red glass pierces the skin of her slender waist and tattoos her stomach with tiny glistening rosebuds of blood. Now she is half-beast, half-woman, eyes of aquamarine flicker in her crocodile head: she is beauty and the beast, the beast is beautiful and it is she. She is female president in the couture house of her dreams, a cyborg goddess dressed in zips that go nowhere, a bloodless Cleopatra swathed in mists of a marshmallow-pink chiffon. She owns the audio and visual interactive rights of her body: sex and love simulations will be sold only to the highest bidder. Already she can give herself to her husband, and not be there at all. 'I will be your playtoy and nothing else.' When he weeps she says, 'Do you want more players to interact with you? Do you want another environment?' She presses D for Dominatrix. E for Erotic simulation. F for Fellatio. N for Nurse (stockings and suspenders under her uniform), S for Spank me and W for Wonderland.

'What new sexual adventure do you want me to design for you, Wilheim?'

'Put your arms around me and kiss me here.' He points to his lips.

Luciana stifles a yawn. 'What text do you want?' Her voice is matter-of-fact like the voice on an ansamachine. 'I want you to say,' he bangs his fist into a pillow, 'say I like you. Say I respect

you. Say you enjoy my company.' She smiles. 'I can be more exciting than that.' Her husband throws himself on to the bed and
buries his face in a pillow so that when he speaks his voice is
muffled. 'Okay, Luciana. I hate you. I despise you.' She nods.
'What's my text, Wilheim?' Her husband thumps the pillow into
his face.

'You moan, you enjoy it, your eyes are closed, your wrists are
tied with red cord, you cry out for me, you cannot have enough
of me, you come, I come, I untie you, we lie in each other's arms
and you admire my body.' Luciana caresses the keyboard with her
long fingers. 'Sometimes it's hard to get my eyes to close,' she
says. 'I'm doing something wrong because technically it's easy.'
And then she laughs and sings in mock-country and western
Tammy Wynette-style, 'Sometimes it's hard to get my eyes to
close.' She does not lift her eyes from the screen.

'I am a voyeur in my own marriage,' Wilheim says.

'But I give my virtual flesh to your fat fingers,' she replies,
motionless in her charcoal silk lingerie, bought with his money.
'It is four in the morning,' she says after a while, closing one file
and opening another. 'Where have you been?'

'Talking to the English woman,' he says. 'And then Tatiana
woke up.'

'I know.'

'If you heard her wake, why didn't you go to her?'

'She wanted you,' his wife replies in her cool no-nonsense
voice.

'I am designing a new interaction for you, Wilheim. You can
have multiple sex partners, how about that? You can fuck ten

woman a night without destroying your mind and soul or taking off your trousers.'

'I want you.'

'You can have me.'

'I want you for real.'

'You can have close-up action and you can have passion,' she mocks and he can hear the Italian in her accent. 'It will be better for you when my technology improves. Soon you will wear gloves that allow you to experience the brush of fingertips and the sting of the whip. You will wear a membrane that simulates human skin over your genitals, and you can joyride to your heart's content.' When he does not reply she says, 'Your fingers smell of sex.'

Her husband bows his head and walks to the bathroom, throwing his tie on the floor. Now she clicks into the nervous system of a zebra and becomes him, stamping her hooves in the dust, slapping flies off her steaming male flanks, looking out at the colourless world with her zebra eyes. She shakes her mane of black hair and walks to the pool of water nearby, lapping it up with her rough tongue. She is a divine thing. She is woman, man and beast, and she is insatiably thirsty.

'Why are you crying?'

When Ben does not reply, Mary lies on her back in the dark and listens to Nancy and Philippe making love next door.

'I thought you were crying for me,' she says finally. 'Why do you pretend to love me when you don't?' She can feel her voice gentle itself and she knows it is because she is asking him to tell her the truth. 'You can keep secrets from me, but you shouldn't keep them from yourself.' The English man inches his body away from hers and she pretends not to notice.

'Stop telling me what I feel.' He hides his hands under the lavender-scented pillow case.

'Chéri chéri chéri chéri chéri!' the American screams and the door of a wardrobe slams.

When Wilheim climbs into bed, Luciana wakes up from her electronic dream, sweating. 'I need water,' she pleads, 'get me some water,' and he does, returning three, four, five times to refill the glass as she shivers and sweats. He feels her pulse and then, satisfied, tries to read the book wedged between the pink folds of his paunch.

It is always at this time of night he hears the Algerian woman shout out what sounds like RabRabRab in her sleep. The German sticks his fingers in his ears. He wants chocolate gâteaux. Girls in bikinis. Male companions to play golf with. He wants to drink beer in friendly taverns and he wants to crack jokes with friends after a good meal. RabRabRab. Wilheim knows that she with the scars on her stomach and golden coins in her ears is in hell and curses her for not suffering quietly.

Rabah Rabah Rabah.

A gendarme pokes his baton into Yasmina's stomach, pushing her backwards. I saw you running, that's what you get for being so pretty. Why are you running so fast, little one? In the distance she can hear sirens and the shattering of glass. I saw you, the gendarme says again. He is a small man. Yes, he is a small man.

What is it that he saw? His breath smells of garlic and wine and he is alone, unsteady on his feet. She leans towards him. Yes. She takes the knife from his back pocket and clasps his hair in her hand. Her fists hit out at his baby face as she slides the knife across his throat. Rabah Rabah Rabah. She kicks the gendarme to the ground and she hears her mother's voice, hard and wounded: You will pick up nail parings with your eyelids in the afterlife. Her brother Omar limps towards her, pointing to the medals he won fighting the Second World War for Europe. Nancy's mother, Jane, says, s'long as you got eyes, a tongue and a throat they'll have you in uniform – hey why do I get stuck inside myself and can't get out again? Just go under? Stuck there, stuck there, it's so goddamn humiliating.

Tatiana sighs and puts the pillow over her head. She is preparing a court case in which she fights for her rights in three languages. In the room next door Claudine sleeps a long untroubled sleep, clutching her teddy bear, the heart in its nylon paw tucked under her chin. Her golden eyelashes flutter against her cheek, which is still warm from the goodnight kisses of eight hours ago. Claudine is kissed into sleep every night. In the morning she wakes up happy and beautiful. Tonight, Biddy Ba Ba lies at the foot of her bed, growling at the blue mist outside.

7

When the Inspector puts the key into his front door he is annoyed to find himself feeling shy. The feeling persists as he watches Luciana's black-blue eyes drag around the floors and walls of his apartment. He hopes he has left no evidence of his private life for her to decipher – his slippers or digestive powders, for example. She sits down on the only armchair and snaps open her snakeskin handbag.

'You smell like the sea, Madame.'

'A woman in Frankfurt makes my perfume, Inspector.' She allows him to light her cigarette and then pushes her wrist under his nose.

'Sea Spray.'

'She is God?' the Inspector jokes, pulling the small wooden chair up next to her and loosening his top button.

'She can make the ocean in seven days.' The Italian woman traces the curve of her eyebrow with her long fingers and he watches her, preoccupied and admiring.

'She makes my sea in a bottle and then I take her to drink apple wine.'

The Inspector watches her rummage in her bag and take out three polaroids.

'But you do not like to eat?' he says.

'I have no appetite.' She smiles, handing him the photographs.

'You have only seen Mary as a corpse. I thought you might like to see her alive?'

Blanc peers at the photographs. Perhaps this flippant, morbid creature is mad, or just bored, with her laboratory ocean scents and crystal pendant reflecting his face back to him every time she changes position on the chair.

'You women are all wearing the same lipstick.' He peers at the first photograph.

She says nothing, flicking the ash from her cigarette into the antique saucer his mother gave him as a wedding present.

'Mary is stroking the English man's hand,' he observes with interest.

'She loathed him,' Luciana replies.

'I don't think so.'

'I know so.'

'I think they will go upstairs and make love.' Blanc looks at the next photograph.

'She didn't like him to touch her.'

'Yes. They will make love. The body does not lie,' he asserts and then stares hard at the polaroid of the unsmiling Italian beauty.

'Oh yes, it does!' She laughs.

He stands up and offers her an aperitif.

'If you mean, Madame, that you have designed your ears, nose, thighs and breasts with the assistance of the excellent Herr Baeur, that is a different thing altogether.' Blanc does not raise his eyes.

'You have done your homework, Inspector,' she eventually says, and her voice is darker, softer.

'Do you often travel in aeroplanes?'

She nods.

'I have heard,' the Inspector lowers his voice confidentially, 'that silicone breasts explode in aeroplanes.'

'But not mine.' She uncrosses her black leather boots, searching for the buttons of her gossamer blouse. The Inspector sighs as she reveals her firm, gently tanned breasts.

'Touch them,' she says in her cool voice, with its strange Italian inflection.

Blanc leans towards her and strokes the dark erect nipple of her left breast.

'Do you know that huge swarms of locusts are devouring crops in North Africa at this moment?' She slips out of the crêpe folds of her skirt. His eyes take in the length of her thighs; she is a sleek unblemished superbreed, svelte, matte, a silvery statue standing on his well-hoovered brown carpet.

'They are having to invent a new pesticide.' She takes his hand and places it on her thigh and he, despite his better judgment, finds it moving over her perfection, exploring contour and form. She bends over and unbuttons his starched white shirt, her fingers searching under his spotless white vest for his armpits, which are sweating.

'Why don't we move into the next room?' she suggests, and he stands up, dizzy with sea spray and the erotic radiance of this robot with breasts, this sculpture with a triangle of golden fur, this vision in unbuttoned silver gossamer, and leads her to his lonely bed, too curious to mind her seeing the glass of water, the small plate with its crust of Brie, the knife and fork neatly placed together, and his alarm clock, all of them arranged on the table next to the bed. He has no time to feel shamed by this evidence of his late-night lonesome snacks because she has pushed him lightly on to the bed and, straddled across his thickening stomach, presses her sex against his.

'Take off your shirt,' he whispers, but she shakes her head.

'I never take off my shirt.' Instead she takes off her pants, and unsmiling says, 'Fuck me,' searching for his penis which is flaccid in her hand. 'Fuck me,' she says again and he turns away, muttering something into the nylon quilt of his bed.

'What did you say?' she asks bewildered. He mutters again.

'I can't hear you.'

'I said, can I put the knife inside you?'

She pauses, bewildered.

'What knife?'

He half-heartedly points to the plate on the side-table by the bed. Luciana picks up the knife, running her hands down the sharp jig-jags of the blade.

'Put the knife where?'

'Let me,' he begs.

The sight of the knife in her hand has excited him. The Inspector pushes against her, moaning and ashamed.

'Let me,' he murmurs again.

'No.'

'Let me.'

He is hard now, struggling with her as he reaches between her legs, one hand pressing against her throat. When the telephone rings she considers picking it up and asking for help.

'I'm sorry.' He eventually picks up the telephone and puts it straight down again, rubbing his chest, not catching her eye.

'I will have that aperitif.' She sleeks down her hair, and then searches for her packet of menthol cigarettes. The room smells of stormy ocean, of rock pools, gulls and salt-encrusted rocks.

'So, Inspector. Tell me what it was like being a young French officer in Algeria.'

'La torture?'

Blanc pours himself a whisky. This time it is he who sits in the armchair while she stands facing him, half-leaning against the door.

'The French sent their sons to keep the tricolour flying in Algeria. In France we said "La guerre d'Algérie". In Algeria they said "the revolution". This grand-style colonial war, Madame, paid my wages, which I sent home to my mother. She understandably hoped for a long war.'

'La torture,' Luciana reminds him.

'I am not frightened of the word. Sometimes there is no choice. Only people with something to hide are secretive, is that not so, Madame?' When he sips his whisky she notices that his hands are shaking. 'The application of psychological and physical pain makes people less secretive. It is however philosophically abhorrent. I'm sure you agree with me.'

'But then, philosophers do not fight wars,' Luciana replies. 'They write about them.'

'Quite so.' Blanc refills his glass. 'I strung up naked Algerians by their feet and plunged their heads into a bucket of water. Later on I improvised a little and placed a spiked steel trestle table underneath the suspect. A little push in the right direction and he would swing past the table, grazing his genitals on the spikes.'

The Italian finds herself staring at a portrait of a middle-aged woman hanging on the wall. Why is it interesting, this amateur attempt in oil paint? The woman looks mild enough in her blue cardigan and pearls. Her features are composed but her eyes are distracted as they stare out at the brown velveteen sofa. Even her hand, which lightly touches the pearl necklace, looks as if it has suddenly been flung up in alarm.

Luciana walks to the table and puts down her glass.

'It is not good for a young man to hear the screams of the tortured,' Blanc continues, casually picking up the polaroids on the table and holding them close to his eyes. 'We would shout "Vive la France! Vive la France!" over their cries until it was over.' He bows his head. 'In some ways you could say it is my wife who has suffered the most for France.'

The Inspector wipes his eyes on the sleeve of his towelling robe and stares morosely at the portrait on his wall. He stares at his bare feet.

'If you find her, tell her I don't like to sleep alone.'

The Italian woman nods, pushing open the door with her thin shoulders.

'Two things,' he calls out to her. 'The photographs. Can I keep them?'

'If they help your enquiry.'

'Oh, they do.' The whisky has deepened his voice. 'You see, although I have seen most of your body, I have not seen you here.' He holds up one of the polaroids.

'There appear to be ants crawling up your arms, Madame. In fact they are track marks.' He smiles. 'I have met a few junkies in my time but none as beautiful as you.'

8

My father's a policeman — clap clap
my brother's a cowboy — clap clap
my uncle's a judge — clap clap

Claudine and Tatiana pretend to stab each other with a pair of scissors.

The Algerian says to the Polish woman, 'Think of an emotion and then hide it. I must see all this in your face and try to guess what it is you are hiding.' The children watch her. Tatiana's lips set into an exact copy of the expression on Monika's face.

'Is it anger?' Yasmina asks.

'No. I am feeling love. I am feeling love and I am hiding it.'

'So.' Yasmina looks down at the cloth Monika is embroidering. 'You look like you are angry with someone when you really love them?'

I'm a pig with a tail like a corkscrew — clap clap.

'Luciana!' Wilheim yells from the kitchen, where he is pricking coils of bulging beef sausage for the evening meal. 'Telephone.'

The pleats of Luciana's black crêpe skirt dip and swirl as she makes her way to the corridor.

'It must be her perfumier. Urgent business,' Wilheim pants, stabbing the meat with relish.

'We should all play Murder in the Dark one night,' the English man suggests, unpacking his accordion. Monika, who has been murdering in the dark all night, changes the subject. 'You must think of an object and I will try and guess what it is just from the expression on your face.' The Algerian chooses a walnut, the English woman a snowstorm in a bottle and the American a tiara. Monika studies Nancy's face. 'It is something hard,' she says. 'Something that shines, like stainless steel.' Philippe cracks a real walnut, cupping it in his hand and squeezing hard. He gives the nut to Yasmina, the imaginary walnut still in her head for Monika to receive. To confuse her she dips the real one into her glass of milk.

The English man plays his accordion and sings, 'I got a brand neeeew pair of shoes.' Nancy sings in harmony with him. She stops. 'I got a new line.' She takes a breath and hums, 'I capture your curls on my pillow.'

'It's a terrible line.' The English woman laughs.

Nancy closes her eyes and bites into a macaroon.

'No. It is warm and timeless.'

The English man sings experimentally, 'I capture your curls on my pillow.'

'That line makes me want to throw up.'

'She's a fucking bitch, your girlfriend,' Nancy whispers to the English man when he leans into her breasts to light her cigarette.

'Why don't we all go for a walk by the sea?' He wonders why the American is clutching her stomach, smoking and coughing at the same time.

Luciana can hear the sizzle of burning fat from Wilheim's sausages as he pours beer over their bursting guts. Beef, spice and beer – the fat man's speciality. She can see her husband in the kitchen, grease on his chin, handkerchief on his knees, chewing on a piece of dark pungent meat while adding up figures on his calculator. For the first time this holiday she suddenly feels homesick for the spacious blue-carpeted rooms of her Frankfurt mansion. 'We are going to the beach,' Wilheim shouts to his wife, licking beer and salt off his fingers. The real-estate businessman who is her husband walks into the corridor, his face flushed from the heat of the oven, and kisses the cold sculpture of her cheek. He is so anxious to show her the sausages he has lovingly prepared that he does not notice her strange eyes are dark with fear as she stares at the telephone.

Claudine climbs on to a boulder covered in seaweed and slides down again on her stomach. Tatiana throws pebbles into the sea. The lovers and loveless walk on the cliffs, wrapped up against the wind. Sea, stone, air. Large empty houses shut up for the winter. Parisians will arrive in the summer, cars laden with food and wine. The loved and loveless with their cats and dogs, towels and magazines and suntan creams filling the empty houses. Opening the shutters and sweeping the floors. Making every day a day to remember, making it safe, making it familiar, not wanting anything too strange to intrude. The making of each day, hauling the hours in, finding a shape for time.

'My stomach hurts,' Nancy confides to Monika.

'Everything hurts,' is the Polish woman's unsympathetic and enigmatic reply. 'At least you have a body to keep you warm at night.'

The tourists eat crêpes and drink cider in a café by the harbour. The children sip hot chocolate and the men play the pinball machines while the women laugh at smutty postcards on a rack in the café. Nancy translates; if a man has a zizi like a frite he will make love like a potato; if you are an amateur fisherman and your wife is sitting naked on a rock, don't mistake her zizi for a sea urchin. The American woman, postcard in her hand, suddenly doubles over and screams in pain. She is helped to a chair by the women, the loved and unloved women who stroke her forehead and massage her shoulders while she clutches her stomach, trembling and pale. The few locals drinking in the café look bewildered and embarrassed. The women walk her to the toilet and take it in turns to make her wads of toilet paper to put between her legs.

'I'm having a miscarriage,' she weeps, 'damn damn damn,' doubling over, squatting on the toilet floor while the women hurry to get more paper, stroking her hair, rubbing the small of her back as she moans and cries out, 'He doesn't respect me, that's why I keep losing them.'

'Nonsense,' the Polish woman says. 'Love and respect have nothing to do with conception.'

'It's true,' Nancy weeps.

'Bollocks.' Mary strokes her hair.

'You know why my eyes shone so?'

Mary shakes her head.

'Because there were two souls shining through them.'

Nancy looks up through her tears and it is true. Her eyes shine with half the lustre of before.

Biddy Ba Ba stays awake all night hissing at stray moths. Claudine has left the window open for him in case he wants to roam in the garden. Before she went to bed she held him in her arms and made him look at the stars, willing him to be brave and explore the frozen land beyond the château. The beast crouches under the table, contemplating the great outdoors with horror. Staring at the stars from his position under the table, the beast does not like the window open. And there is too much space between each star. Absolutely nothing, not love nor nature, reassures Biddy Ba Ba that outside is a good place to be. He pulls off the coffee-coloured wing of the largest moth and then steps back to watch it suffer.

When the early morning breeze spins the globe into Acapulco, Honduras and Managua, and the grandfather clock in the marble tiled hall chimes seven times, Nancy throws out the thirteen eggs. The secret voodoo she put in the fridge when she first arrived. She drops them into a black bin-liner one by one, listening to them splash, ties up the bag and carries it to the bins at the end of the drive where Biddy Ba Ba cringes near the empty letter box. She puts her hand through the rusting flap just to see if there might be a message, a postcard from 'outside.' When there is not, she hugs the cat to her chest, lips pressed against the tiger fur of his head. Someone taps her on the shoulder and the American woman knows exactly who it is. Without turning round she says, 'Tell me about my mother.'

'Yes,' Yasmina replies. 'I came to find you.'

They walk back to the house, Nancy sobbing and clutching the cat. Yasmina points to the trees.

'Lovers like to carve their initials into the bark of the cedar because it is soft.' Nancy looks at the blur of trees through her tears and hallucinates her maverick father, penknife in his big hands, cutting the words 'Jane and Jim 4ever' into the soft bark. Sap runs, insects hum, birds sing. His wife carries four-year-old Nancy in her arms, smiling, shy when she sees the love words. He says something corny like 'If I had an aeroplane I'd skywrite us, honey, but I only have a knife.' The sun is shining and their arms are brown. Nature, Culture, Love, Children. Nancy weeps and weeps.

Princess Tatiana sits alone in the kitchen, reading her book in the early morning light. A silver crown sits askew on her head and she has half-heartedly pulled the taffeta dress over her pyjamas. When Biddy Ba Ba jumps on to her lap she beats him with her cardboard wand until he wails. She drinks a glass of milk and ignores Yasmina and Nancy when they sit at the large table, five places away from her.

'Okay,' Yasmina begins, as she has done so many times before.

'What do we already know?'

'My mother's name was Jane. My father's name was Jim. She was a writer, he was a scientist.'

'They lived in Tangier where you were born,' Yasmina continues.

'Yes.'

'Jane shot herself.'

'Yes.'

'What else do we know?'

'You knew my father's friend?'

'Jack.'

'How did you know him?'

'I will have to go back to eighteen thirty, the year France colonised Algiers, to tell you.'

Nancy sighs. 'I just want to know about her.'

Yasmina smiles. 'What are you reading, Tatiana?'

The child holds up her book, an Italian, French and English dictionary.

'Why are you learning these languages?'

'Why do you think?' Tatiana takes a long considered sip of her milk. 'I want to be understood in all of them.'

'So there's Jim and Jane and Jack and you,' Nancy persists.

'That's half the story.'

'Who else?'

'Safia, Rabah, Omar, my mother, Ahmed, Doctor Paranoid.'

'And you?' The princess interrogates the citizens who have invaded her early morning domain.

'Yes.'

The American holds up her hand. 'Just make me happy and connect me up to my folk,' she sighs.

'Sure.' Yasmina fiddles with her golden earrings. 'We'll start in Tangier when Jim your father and Jack his friend walked to the taxi rank looking for a couple of whores.'

PART TWO

9

Tangier 1957. Two men lean against a taxi, taking us in with their blue eyes. All muscle and white teeth. The taller one slips his hand under his belt and whispers something to his friend in the white T-shirt. They jingle coins in their sunburnt fists. Yes. We walk towards them.

Ahmed is trying to sell the Americans hardboiled eggs. Earlier this morning Safia saw him peeling the skin off little fish that had fallen on to the pavement by the docks. Stuffing them into his big hungry mouth. So where did he get the eggs from? Right now the men have turned their backs on us and are choosing an egg. The one in the white T-shirt cracks the shell on Ahmed's shaved head and shouts, 'Tune in!' His friend laughs, all the time shaking his head. He lights up a cigarette and blows out the smoke, excited.

It is not a good idea to crack an egg on a head full of ringworm. In fact, it is not a good idea to crack an egg on this boy's head at all. Ahmed knows how to make bombs. The men chew their eggs slowly, eyes squinting in the sun.

'Hi. What's your name?'

'Linda.' Safia's voice is like her face. Melancholy and deadpan. 'My name's Jim.' He opens the door of the taxi and gets in first, followed by Safia and then myself. The man in the white T-shirt jumps into the front and slams the door.

'Yahoo!' He fiddles with the gears and grins at the driver who winds down the window. The cab fills with the sound of birds screeching in the trees.

Safia looks out of the window at men from the country being shaved on the street. Flies settle on her long hands. She has roamed through forests and caves dressed as a man, her pockets full of white feathers the doves of Kabylia leave on rocks, but now she sits dead still, as she always does after she's smoked kif. She keeps it in a linen pillowcase a French woman gave to her mother. Jim stares at the plastic sandals poking through the cloth of her peppermint-coloured kaftan.

'Think she's alive?'

His friend turns round and steals a glance over his shoulder.

'Pinch her.'

Jim pinches Safia's arm. 'Hey Linda? Lin-da? Li-nnnn-da! What were you two girls talking about when you were walking to the taxi stand?'

Safia doesn't flinch. She's longing for a smoke and a can of milk.

Jack takes out a small brown notebook and writes something down. He turns his head sideways to me.

'Got a name, sweetheart?'

'Jane.'

He grins at the driver who is fiddling with the radio tuner, two damp circles under his arms.

'Got any jazz for Jane-y?' He offers him a cigarette.

'Americano. Very good.'

News from Algiers. *The French paras broke up the general strike at the end of January. Shops closed and shuttered. No post or telegraph. Jeeps prowl streets, urging strikers back to work through loud speakers.* The driver turns up the volume, smoking his American cigarette. *Army helicopters drop leaflets on the casbah. Children watch the French drive tanks into shopfronts. Food spills on to the streets.*

'The sky's weird here, man, it's green at night. Why've you got green skies eh, Linda?' Jim prods her knee. Safia's bloodshot eyes fix on the cracks in pavements. *Oranges, bananas, honey cakes*, the words crackle through the radio just as the taxi swerves to avoid a dog that suddenly runs into the road. Not fast enough.

The driver slams his brakes down and blood sprays the windscreen. Shocked, he curses the yowling dog running in demented circles under the car.

'Do you believe in portents?' Jim says.

'Huh?'

'Well.' Jim cradles his forehead in his big hands. 'You know, that dog's out of control. Chasing its tail.' He looks at me and lowers his voice. 'It freaks me out that she's called Jane.'

'Why?'

'Cause my Janey, she's going crazy back home. She's out of control, Jack.'

'Shit.' The American thinks for a while. 'Jane will be okay.'

'No man. She's weird. I mean, I'm a science man, right?'

'Right.'

'What I was going to say is, I have to go into black holes and

75

get myself back to earth again. But Jane! She's floating somewhere inside those holes and she can't get back.'

'Doesn't sound like the sweet Jane I know.'

'And I can't find the formulae to bring her back.' Jim thumps his chest. 'To me, Jack. To bring her back to me.'

The driver is wiping the windscreen with his handkerchief.

'Know what she did the other day?'

'What?'

'She was putting some lotion on her hands. And she's reading what's in this damn lotion, you know, written on the back of the bottle, and she says in this scary voice, "Why Jim. Did you know Allantoin is good for cell renewal?" '

The driver climbs back into his seat and starts the car.

The room is small and cool with a little bed in the corner neatly made up. A wooden table stands next to it, bare, just a candle and ashtray. The American opens the glass doors and walks out on to a balcony overlooking the sea. He puts his hands on his hips, staring at the ocean, and breathes out, very soft. 'Wow.' A beacon flashes on and off, splashing red light on to his face. We can hear the American expats talking downstairs, their voices thick with opium and whisky. He walks back into the room and I follow him, waiting while he unties the laces of his boots and then throws them on to the floor. 'Oh boy.' He collapses on to the bed, arms behind his neck.

'Y'know, the girls I usually date . . . they're called things like Ellen and Sarah-Lou. They wear ribbons in their hair, toast marshmallows by the fire and read the funnies on Sunday.' He reaches over and lights the candle on the desk. 'Sarah-Lou,' he says again, dragging his lips across the words. He blows out the match and looks at me sideways.

'Know what I want right now? A bowl of cereal! Say . . . um . . . little darlin', why don't you take the weight off your feet?' He pats the bed with his big hands.

'Want a cigarette?'

'No.' I lie.

'Hey – you spoke!'

The smell of opium drifts in through the gap under the door. The American breathes deeply and pats his stomach. 'My mother's name is Marie. My folk go back to Breton, see.' His finger, yellow from nicotine, traces my lips.

'Whooooo.' He whistles through his teeth. 'You're only a baby!' His blue eyes flicker across my stomach and breasts. Weighing up the sum of what he has seen. The American has bought damaged goods.

'When I was sixteen I was soccer crazy. Do Arab boys play?' His lips stretch into a smile, or it could be disgust, because his mouth freezes for a while, teeth bared, slits of blue where his eyes are crinkled, as if he is looking up into a blinding sun. 'Marie. That's my blessed mom's name. You like that name? French, see.' He stubs out his cigarette and lights another.

'Marie. Pretty, huh? That's a virgin name.'

10

Sétif 1945. Daughters are meant to love their mothers but I hate mine. I am five years old and she is ill, as she always is, lying in bed suffering. There's dust in my eyes. I'm sitting on a chair by her bed and she is pinching me. It helps the pain, she says, but she is smiling. So I smile back and she pinches me harder, finger and thumb tightening on the skin of my arm. I am crying and smiling at the same time, and she is in pain and smiling at the same time. I don't know what part of the pinch is love, what part of the pinch is pain, and I can't tell anyone she's hurting me because then I would betray the part that is love.

When my uncle tried to get her into the European hospital, she refused, preferring the amulets, resins and potions women make in the villages nearby to the foreigners' penicillin. 'I know how to get into the hospital but I don't know how to get out – the Europeans will keep me there and kill me.' When they gave her pills she swallowed the lot in one dose. 'If it doesn't cure me in one gulp it's no good.' More intimate with pain than love, she understood its strokes, knew how to hurt without appearing to do so.

'The white doctors in their hospitals in the cities – why should they be tender with my body? Why would they want to relieve me of stomach rot?' Sometimes when the pain left her body she would curse my father, her voice hard, wounded. 'A man is like the hands of a clock. His penis points in all directions.' Now she is pinching me again. 'The butcher was good to pregnant women. He gave me anything I wanted. Liver and all the internal organs of a freshly slaughtered sheep. So you were born with a piece of liver between your teeth.' Yesterday, when she cut my fingernails she told me that if I was bad I would have to pick up the nail parings with my eyelids in the afterlife.

The colonial doctor, a fat breathless man with very clean hands, came to the house to give her vitamin injections once a month. He sold them in three sizes, small for one hundred francs, medium for five hundred, and large cost fifteen hundred. My mother paid him with money she stole from my father's pocket.

Rabah, my uncle, great lover of metropolitan cities, arrived one day while he was injecting her. If my mother troubled me, my uncle, who lived half the year in Algiers and the other half in Europe, thrilled me. Dressed in a linen suit bought in Rome and a heavy gold watch bought in Egypt, he watched the doctor curiously, arms folded over his sharp lapels, fingers stained with a mixture of his two trades: ink and flour. Rabah is a baker and a journalist. His most famous article for the newspapers was the one about words: how the Vichy régime replaced the slogan of the French revolution, Liberté, Egalité, Fraternité, with the words Family, Homeland and Work. His most famous cake was the one he iced in the style of the American artist Jackson Pollock, whom Rabah met when he was working in New York. He told me about the giant seventeen-foot canvases, how the artist standing above them in his studio on Long Island, legs akimbo, used a stick to paint with, waiting for the right moment to make a move. My uncle's voice, lazy, gentle and amorous.

If he loved the cities, it was the countryside that gave him health and made him handsome. The orange blossom in May, the wild absinthe that scents the air near the coast, and the winds that blow from the Sahara. But now Rabah has his arms folded, watching the liquid inside the syringe disappear into my mother's arm. 'Monsieur Docteur' . . . There is menace in his voice as he suddenly pulls the syringe out of the doctor's hands, takes off his sunshades and examines it. 'Salt!' he shouts. 'What are you doing injecting her with salt serum?' The doctor, caught out, denies it, saying he packed his bag with the wrong medicines that day, but it turns out he has been filling her body with salt all the time and not vitamins. A landowner from Liège, he has become very rich out of the likes of my mother. Rabah says to the French man, 'There's a party in Paris right now. Why aren't you there? Drinking champagne now we have helped you kick the Germans out.' The doctor just stares. Rabah, who smells of roses, takes out a green handkerchief, sprinkles a few drops of cologne on to it and wipes his forehead. 'Y'know what's happening in San Francisco?' He drags out the words, San Fran-cis-co. The doctor taps the toe of his little black polished boot, impatient, edgy. He has come to the house of a poor illiterate woman, not expecting the intervention of a maverick educated uncle in a suit smarter than his own.

'The *colons* have got pens in their hands, Monsieur Docteur. What for? Eh? Any idea, Monsieur? They are signing the United Nations Charter declaring the rights of subject peoples to self-determination.' My mother is pinching me again, not knowing what's happening – just seeing her brother talking quietly to the doctor who is packing up his bag. 'If the French are celebrating getting rid of the jackboots in their country, what the hell are you doing in ours?'

Mr Clean Hands took a long look at my handsome uncle – his suit, his shades, his shoes – and then he said something strange. Pointing his plump forefinger at Rabah, jabbing out each word, he said, 'You're mine,' snapped his bag shut and left the house.

When I went to the beach on holidays with my uncle, I would watch the French settlers, the *colons*, splash in the water all day. They are Mediterraneans and love the sea. My uncle liked to look inland towards the heart of Africa, preferring the mountains and desert oases. The old women *colons* sat on park benches in the shade, knitting and gossiping while their men took a siesta, but the younger ones danced under the stars at night in summer dresses. Jiving and flirting in bright clothes, flicking their pony-tails and swinging ther hips on the warm night-time sand. What were they going to be when they grew up? What was I going to be when I grew up?

If Monsieur Docteur injected my mother with salt, my uncle injected me with modernity. That is how he corrupted me. It was he who injected Europe into my life, passed on to me the hybrid virus of the English language, atheism, American slang, Mickey Mouse, and once he bought me a glass jar of marmalade. He taught me odd Russian phrases picked up on his travels, curious words like cannibal, traitor, cholera, purge. He also bought me biros and exercise books, taught me the names of painters, movie stars and pop singers.

No wonder women told him their thoughts like they told no other man. Rabah admired their bodies and laughed at their jokes. He looked like what he was, a desired and much loved man with light in his eyes and money in the bank. But he also hurt women. I have seen them weep over Rabah because he removed his affection and attention and the light in his eyes shone on someone else. How was it that he could love me one day and not love me the next? What do you do with the love you feel if it is not returned?

'What's wrong, Uncle?'

'Politics.'

I did not understand, but his perfume made me daydream long after my mother finished pinching me. The morning he caught out Clean Hands and his salt serum injections was Victory Day. VE Day. The day my brother O limped home to drought and famine and dust, French medals pinned on his chest.

O lost his leg for Europe. Fighting with the French. He says in France the épiceries are empty – everything has been plundered by the Germans and everyone wants to sleep. He has heard that the yankee airmen, returning home, knelt down and kissed the

US soil. Please don't talk to him, he never wants to talk again. Rabah helps him out of his uniform, massaging his shoulders, squeezing his hand, and O's eyes are closing. My mother gets out of bed, boils him bread with lemon and oil, climbs back into bed. He eats and gets some strength, so we all sit with him, waiting for him to come back to himself. He gives me a colouring-in book, pictures of Red Sea fishes, but it is my uncle who reads me their names: the masked butterflyfish, the reef stingray and the scalefin that feeds on small shrimps, porcupine and parrot fish. I have to colour them in with crayons, O says. But I haven't got any crayons. Rabah takes something out of his jacket pocket. A lipstick. Pink. My mother wants it, she is holding out her thin hands, crying, 'Give it to me, give it to me!' I start to colour the Hawkfish pink.

'You-you-you, give it to me!' but I will not. I hold on to the pink colour, watching her pale lips bleat you-you-you – her pained eyes fixed on my hands. She is so thin I can feel her hips through the bedcovers. Something is happening outside.

you-you-you

The roads are filling with bicycles, taxis, even horses. We can hear the women ululating – you-you-you. Where are they? There has been no rain for months. People are edgy. Shadowy figures move through clouds of dust, handkerchiefs over their mouths. Children fight with dogs for garbage. Men are pouring into the streets from the outskirts. We hear the chanting – LONG LIVE A FREE AND INDEPENDENT ALGERIA. O limps into the crowd with his crutch. Uncle takes my hand, he holds on tight to me as we follow my brother. The gendarmes point their guns at the men who are holding banners and green and white flags. They shoot into the sky but no one takes any notice. There are so many of us. A French commissaire marches comically into the crowd and tries to take down a banner. The people start to stone him and he beats them off with his walking stick, swearing in French. More police. Men are still pouring into the square, holding banners, shouting, fists raised in the dust swirling above their heads. A man in uniform comes out of a café wiping his mouth. Long Live a Free and Independent Algeria. The chanting is swelling under the yellow sky. He reaches for his gun and shoots. I've still got the lipstick in my hand, and then, bang, the guns are firing, people falling, screaming. Banners and flags are splashed with blood as the guns fire, on and on. We wait for them to stop but they do not stop. My uncle pulls at me, trying to get me home, but a man in uniform jumps on him and drags him to the ground. I see a stick come down on Rabah's head. When he covers it with his hands they beat his hands. My brother finds me. I hold on to him as we limp through bodies on the ground.

O pulls me into an alleyway. More dust. Chicken bones. Two gendarmes come towards us swinging batons. They beckon to him to hurry up. He cannot walk faster so he shouts that he has just come back from France, fighting for France. One of the gendarmes chucks me under the chin. 'Ma chouchou.' The other pulls my brother's trousers down. I can see the half-stump of his leg. Then they pull his underpants down and bend over him with the knife, my brother on the ground screaming, 'I have medals, you gave me medals, let the girl go.' The gendarmes look strange, their eyes bright, a flush in their cheeks. He looks up at me. 'Is this your brother?' I nod. Why is the dust wet? O's mouth is open. Wide open.

11

Jack unzips his jeans. 'I'm just a country boy without a dollar and I'm pleased to see you.' Five cigarette butts burn in the ashtray.

The small candle spits yellow wax. 'Whoooo baby let's go!'

He walks over in his shorts and presses against me.

Someone is knocking on the door but he ignores them, eyes half-shut.

Bang Bang Bang.

'Who's there?'

'Me.' It's a woman's voice. American.

'Who's me?'

'Me!'

'Shit.' The American thumps his fist into his thigh.

The door opens and he pulls away from me as a tall slender woman in slacks and sandals walks into the room, a large brown book tucked under her arm.

'Well. He-llo.'

'Hi, Jane . . . look . . . '

'No. I'm not gonna come back later.' She sits down on the small wooden chair and lights a cigarette, one long leg crossed over her knee. 'Damn you, Jack.' She blows out smoke, eyes flickering towards me.

'I want some fun, Janey. I was on that ship for a long time.' He sits on the edge of the bed and searches for a cigarette.

'Damn you, Jack.'

'What do you mean damn you?'

The woman takes out a bottle of pills, drops two into her mouth and chews.

'Codeine.' She smiles.

'Get out of here, Jane.'

For a moment she looks startled. We can hear the drugged voices of the men downstairs. They are singing and banging on tables.

'Thought I heard Jim's voice,' she says softly. Jack looks uncomfortable. He points to his tanned legs and pale ankles.

'See how white my feet are? Gotta put 'em in the sun so they match.'

'Just wanted to say hi, Jack. Heard you were in town.'

'Yeah, well, we can say hi some other time, okay?'

'Is that right?' She taps the brown leather book resting in her lap.

'I brought my photo album, Jacky.' She is smiling again but her eyes are sad. 'Thought we could look over ol' America.' Her voice is hard. 'Memories, Jack. Y'know, when we were teenagers?'

'Jeez, Jane, don't you have eyes in your head?' He rolls his eyes towards me.

'Sure. Think I've done a reading of the general situation.'

'But you aren't hip to the situation, Jane. How many codeine you had today?'

She opens the book. 'Just need to get a grip on things. Like who the hell I am.' She looks at me, suddenly shy. 'And who the hell is she, Jacky?' Her fingernail, painted with pearl varnish, points at me and then runs down a photograph, teasing. 'See this picture, here . . . at the Cherokee Indian reservation? Me and my little brother standing beside this guy in his feather headdress? There's the stall with the postcards . . . and here,' her blonde head bends over the book, 'summertime in Long Island. The sprinklers are out in the garden and we're running about in our little bathing suits. Man, here's that picnic on the beach at Sarasota!'

'Look, Jane, I don't want to see this. I want you to go.' He slides his big hands under her arms, trying to lift her up from the chair.

'Give me three minutes, Jack, okay?'

'And then you'll go?'

'Sure.'

'Okay.'

He stands next to her chair, leaning against the wall in his shorts, arms folded, looking down at the photo album.

'Jacky? What about this one? I'm lining up at the movie theater to see *Gone with the Wind*. Here's little old me feeding nickels into the jukebox to hear Bonnie Baker's "Oh, Johnny, Oh!" Look, I'm wearing bobbysocks, man! That's my date in the sodashop! Remember Teddy? He's the guy that wore the zoot suit. Remember the roller rink, Jacky?'

'Okay, Jane. I'm looking at my watch now and you've got another two minutes.'

'I want to talk about my mom.'

Jack whistles. 'Fine. Talk about your mom for two minutes.'

'Here she is. Remember her? Making damn sure every hour of her life is filled in case she ever has to think? Eating cake. No, not *eating* cake. Devouring cake. Fighting communism from the suburbs. She joined all those clubs. Look at her, atoms for peace and all that shit. I never wanna be like her . . . never never never.'

'No, Janey. You're nothing like her.'

'Cupcakes and teaparties, then there's the shopping, the hairdresser, and bridge. Want to see her?'

She's talking to me. I don't answer, I don't even look at her. I keep my eyes down, staring at the stone floor. But something makes me look. I have to look. Straight into the miserable eyes of a portly woman in a hat and white gloves. She stands by an American soldier, a young boy, both of them smiling out of the photograph at me.

'She wears gloves in the broiling daytime and she's always at some committee meeting.'

'Time to go, Jane.'

'Yeah. That's my brother after he got called up, there he is! Mister Brawny. As long as you've got eyes, a tongue and a throat they'll have you in uniform. But see, Jack, you do get perks . . . y'know, goverment toiletries. You get a slab of Lux, you get towels and a handkerchief and a winter uniform, 'cause the American GI, he is the best equipped soldier in the whole wide world. He gets a tent, a bayonet, a raincoat, a first-aid pouch and he dies!

Yep, my brother died a well-dressed man. Hey, you remember how Superman pushed the Red Cross and V Bonds in the comics? I don't know who took this one. Who's that?' She points and looks up at the American.

'Frank Albert Sinatra.' Jack yawns.

'Don't know how this got here. Yeah I do. He was playing at the Paramount Theater . . . on Columbus Day? Blue eyes like your blue eyes.'

'He's a square.' Jack fiddles with a strand of her blonde hair.

'Yeah. Know what Robert Sylvester said about squares?'

'Who?'

'He's a writer. Like me . . . and he said the square always carries a hanky with his initials embroidered on it. He puts vermouth in his martini, he doesn't rip the bands off his cigars when he has a smoke, he doesn't tip in restaurants and he takes his portable radio to the ball game so he can follow the score.'

'Who gives a fuck what Sinatra puts in his martini. Bye, Jane.'

'And all the high school kids swooning for Frank, carried away on stretchers.'

'Why are you telling me this shit?'

'Because, well, I'd quite like to be carried away on a stretcher just like them, Jacky.'

'What's happening to you, Jane?'

She ignores him.

'Yeah, it's coming back – that TV psychiatrist said it was Frankie's weedy build that brought out the maternal instinct of the female population. Like the women wanted to feed the hungry, and Frank was hungry!'

'One minute left.'

'Oh boy, Jack, here we are, you and me, eating ice-cream! You got melba peach and I got tutti frutti and I want to be Rita Hayworth. Do you remember Ava Gardner in *The Hucksters*? Jack, I've got so much of America in this book! So much, man—I could've been Miss Grill. Miss Grill of Maryland. With a crown of frankfurters and a little pink apron. Thank God I got out, thank God I met Jim, even though it's hard here but I guess it's kind of hard everywhere.'

'Yeah. It's kind of hard everywhere. See ya later.'

'Like, everyone's wrecked in this town. Jim thinks he's an agent sent from another planet.'

'UP UP UP.' He's tipping up her chair and she's hanging on, talking while he tries to slide her off.

'There's no one to talk to here. Y'know, just sweet ordinary talk. Like what are you thinking about these days? Been on any good walks? What pizza do you like to eat, had any good visions? Are you in love like you want to be – that's what you said? What did you get for your birthday, where do you buy your socks, do you like the new way I do my hair? Do you think I look OKAY?'

'Yeah, you look OKAY, Jane. Get out of here!'

'But I don't FEEL okay.' She is shouting at him now. He looks away. Her voice comes back, soft and cajoling, her eyes fixed on the small candle spluttering from the breeze coming through the door.

'Get out of here, Jane!'

'Like you could ask me what I am doing for money, where do the kids go to school, do I still love Jim and how do I most want to live my life and how do you most want to live your life? Why do I sometimes just feel bleak, so bleak I can't look after the kids or talk to Jim? Humiliating. It's so GODDAMN humiliating. There's no such thing as paradise, Jack, there just isn't. It's so damn sad to lose your dream. Don't know what mine is any more.' She turns to me.

'You got a dream?'

'She doesn't speak English, Jane.' The American pulls up his shorts.

'Jack, why do I go into myself and can't get out again? Just go under, stuck there, stuck there, stuck there, stuck there, goddamn you, Jack! I wanted to talk to you about getting older, I wanted to talk to you about dignity.'

She stands up and turns away from us now, crying, but trying not to. Hand in her blonde hair, she looks through the glass doors on to the sea.

'Look, Jane, we'll talk this evening, okay?'

'Yeah.' She brushes a fly off her cheek. She is slender in her sandals, lightly tanned. Her eyes meet his blue gaze and then quickly look away.

'Hey, you?' She is talking to me again. Her voice dark, gentle.

'What's your name?'

'Jane.'

'Is that so?' She half-smiles. 'Isn't that a coincidence? Well, goodbye Jane.'

She turns to Jack. 'I didn't just bring my photo album.' Her hands slide inside the lemon silk of her blouse. 'I've got a present for you.'

Her fingers tug at something. The beacon flashes a strip of green light over the American's thick neck.

She takes out a small revolver, stroking its tortoise-shell handle with her pearly fingers.

'For you, bad boy.' She presses it into his hands.

'God, Jane.'

'I'm scared I might use it on the kids,' she says in her velvety American voice.

She begins to walk quietly out of the room, and stops.

'Did you pack a medical kit? You do when you've got kids. Band-aids. Antiseptic cream. Thermometer. Insect repellent, anti-malarial tablets.'

She walks out and shuts the door.

'Jesus.' He stares at the gun, mouth screwed up, shaking his head.

'I used to carry my kitten like this,' he says, walking with it to the table by the bed, putting it down very gently by the flickering candle.

12

The French entered Algeria in 1830. They claim they made a country out of nothing. What is nothing? That is what I ask Rabah. My father disappeared. One night he did not come home. Is he nothing? I was born under a vast sky in a land of blistering rocks. Was I born into nothingness? When the French military look at me, what do they see? I am here but I am not here at the same time. Like my mother. When she died I moved to Algiers to live with my uncle. She was buried in Sétif and mint grows over her grave. Perhaps one day I will go back to Sétif and talk to her nothingness. But now I am fourteen and have no words for her.

I do have words for her.

I love you. I hate you.

Rabah says there is a word that describes my feelings. He says he would like me to at least try to speak. When the chergui blows from the Sahara it stings the eyes and chokes the breath. That is the feeling in my body when I think about my brother and mother. Last night I dreamt I was trying to pick up nail parings with my eyelids. I lay on my side, cheek close to the floor, eyelashes fluttering across the tiny sliver of nail, my fist bunched into my heart.

This morning I eat Rabah's delicately flavoured dates and ask him questions. Rabah watches me grow into my fourteen years with pleasure and curiosity because he has no daughter of his own. But I think he just likes me anyway.

It is with his dark eyes, irreverent and troubled, that I look at the world I find myself in. With his gaze and not that of the French administrators, governors, judges, technical advisers and tax inspectors. No. I lie. I do look with their eyes. I have had to learn to look with their eyes, in particular the eyes of the young gendarmes who cut into the body of my brother. I watch them watching me. I translate myself to myself via them. That is how the French Presence is inside my body. Two days before the Catholic *pieds-noirs* were preparing their celebrations for All Saints' Day, my brother Omar, who is dead, walked into Rabah's apartment.

Rabah is baking. His apartment warm with the heat and smell of bread. It is built in the French style with large windows and a balcony. There are no courtyards. The courtyard is female space, space that is directed inwards, space that is within. Masculine space is directed outwards, towards the streets. So when I go on to the balcony I am violating a code of movement. I am trespassing male space. But then I am a trespasser. I have been corrupted.

So, what is Nothingness? Rabah only says, 'Yasmina, why are you hungry all the time?' I shrug. He is baking something special today. 'Let me tell you what is happening in France,' he says.

'The French people, in France that is, imagine they can see flying saucers in the sky.' He moves the bowl of dates away from my fingers. 'They go out for their early evening walk, and there one is! Glowing in the French sky is a sphere of strangeness! They eat at cafés in small provincial towns and everything seems normal enough. The steak. The vegetables. Good wine. By the time they order their Calvados and coffee, the unspeakable has happened. A flying saucer is spinning above their heads! They are being invaded by extraterrestrials, Yasmina. Aliens are interrupting the meals they worked hard to buy. Aliens are landing in their corn fields and making strange codes with the crops. The farmers do not understand their language. There are plans to bribe some alien collaborators who will translate these codes and inform French Intelligence of extraterrestrial strategy. Office workers maybe get a little bored at work and look out of the window. What do they see? Strangers dancing on the edge of a spinning sphere! They call the boss. The boss shakes his head and says something must be done about it. And let us not forget the lovers. Lovers walk hand in hand down the boulevards of Paris. They feel uneasy. When they kiss, alien eyes watch their bodies. They are an occupied people. A strange and alien presence has settled in the very centre of the French people. Every small thing the French do is observed. They find themselves getting secretive and sly. It is an invasion of the street, the bathroom and the psyche.'

The telephone is ringing. Rabah, carried away, ignores it.

'Already existentialists are writing articles about this alien presence over a glass of red wine in cafés. Finally a hero, a chef at one of the leading restaurants in Paris, flings up his arms . . .'

'The telephone, Rabah.'

'I know, I know, so the chef puts the last spoonful of mustard into the pepper sauce, flings up his arms and shouts, "Call in the Secretary of State for Air." ' Rabah runs to the telephone.

'No no chérie.

'Yes okay. Everything fine.

'Hmmm.

'I will be in New York on the Seventh.'

My uncle is murmuring lovethings in English.

I have long known that Rabah slips from one world to another, small suitcase in his hand, Egyptian watch on his wrist. Zones and borders are atmospheres, he says, and insists that sometimes he is invisible. An invisible man inside an atmosphere. Because he is not mystical or religious in any way, I do not understand. Perhaps he means that for some reason he is unseen, unperceived, because he is too vain to be invisible. Why else would he have aromatic perfumes specially made for him?

Everything is fine, sweetheart.

*

Why does Rabah lie to his women? I know, and he knows, there is going to be trouble on All Saints' Day. Recently, in the Constantine region, when the European mine masters came home at noon to have lunch with their wives, the mine workers attacked the village. European women had their bellies slashed with sticks and knives.

Algiers has been divided into six zones. All six zones on November the First will attack French police stations and military bases.

Yes, I'll try and bring you a carpet.

In Aurès, where people live on stones and air and rain turns the soil to yellow mud, they are going to attack the French garrison town at Batna.

I try to imagine America. Who is she? Will she kick off her shoes and curl up on the carpet Rabah brings for her, watching the advertisements on television with her pale eyes? I finish Rabah's dates, all the time listening to his conversation, and then I see something that startles me. It belongs to my mother. A box pushed under a chair is covered with the cloth of her wedding dress. It is as if my mother is in the room. Rabah is still on the telephone so I move towards the box.

I am walking towards my mother.
　But she is dead.

*

I love you, Rabah murmurs into the telephone.

I love you. I hate you. Perhaps Rabah cut off her long black hair after she died and keeps it coiled in the box? My heart beats hard at the thought of such a spectacle. What about my father? He disappeared. Perhaps there are papers in the box that will tell me where he is? Do I want to find him? Yes. No. That is ambivalence. I lift up the wedding cloth my mother married him in.

We'll have to get you a winter coat, Rabah whispers.

No. There is not a ghostly coil of black hair in the box. Nor are there documents that will lead me to my absent troubled father. There are guns in the box.

'Yasmina? Where were we?' Rabah finds me bent over the silk sleeves of the wedding dress, counting his weapons. He has a strange light in his eyes.

'Thirteen,' I say.

'Those are good pistols. German mausers abandoned by the Vichy French.' He acts as if it is the most normal thing in the world to have weapons in a box under the chair.

'Can you smell my bread? Where were we?' He lights a cigarette. I know that he is wondering how I feel about the dress, because he only smokes when he is uncomfortable.

'Flying saucers in Provence, Paris and Orléans. In other words, Yasmina, the French are edgy. The psychic state of the French is troubled.'

'Who is she?' I ask.

He gestures to the telephone.

'Oh, a friend. We need all the friends we can get.'

Rabah presses his fingers into the bread and slams the oven doors. 'Okay. Yasmina, because I am your uncle and in charge of your education, I must tell you what is happening in Algeria. Boys like your brother are making bombs in tins of jam.'

And that is when my brother walked into Rabah's apartment. Omar. No, Rabah says gently. He is not Omar.

Rabah brings in the bread. He places it on a cloth. The boy, my uncle and myself stare at the three letters he has made from dough.

F.L.N. Front de Libération Nationale.

I eat the L, Rabah eats the F and the boy eats the N. Rabah points to the thirteen pistols. 'In England,' he says, chewing the bread slowly, 'they call that a baker's dozen.' So, in 1954, when the French went flying-saucer mad, we celebrated the birth of our liberation movement in Rabah's apartment. And my mother was in the room with us, too. The guns wrapped in her wedding cloth, as if inside her belly.

'By the way,' Rabah says to the boy, 'if you blow up the telephone exchange, I won't be able to call my girlfriend.' And then he leaves the room.

*

The boy says, my name is Ahmed. But that is not my only name. He points to his chest. Listen to the jackal.

What is the jackal?

Ahmed says, these are its words:

I am a genius. So why do I sell cabbage heads at the market? Why do I polish shoes on the street? My mother twisted the neck of my newborn sister because she was crying for food. My sister was a genius. She knew how to yell for what she needed. My mother was a genius. She knew how to make carpets. Her feet were mashed in the factory because they did not give her boots. She limped in the hot mash of soap and sodium and her toes became pulp. When I was young I saw French officers slap the cheeks of my grandmother. My grandmother was a genius. She understood that herbs could calm the pain in her cheek. My father was gassed on the Western Front. He was a genius. He knew how to make clay stoves and trays for breadmaking. He knew how to make things grow from stones.

Ahmed chews his bread slowly.

I know every inch of the alleys of the casbah. My casbah is a labyrinth of secret passages leading from one house to another. My casbah has false walls. Inside the walls are bomb factories, caches and hiding-places.

My name is Avenger. Ahmed smiles at me.

*

After a while I say, my name is Avenger too.

'This is Doctor P,' Rabah interrupts us, his arm around the shoulders of a young man carrying a briefcase in one hand and a hatbox in the other.

'My throat hurts,' Ahmed says.

'Give the doctor a break, Ahmed,' Rabah chides.

'What if I die, eh, Rabah?' Ahmed makes a fist with his hand.

'Then you will smell even worse than you do now.'

The man's small hands feel Ahmed's throat. I look away.

'Nothing wrong with you,' he says, and starts to say something to them both about anti-tetanus vaccines, all the time looking at me. Rabah brings in sugar for the doctor's tea.

'Yasmina's mother died at the hands of colonial doctors,' he says, pointing at me. 'He gave my sister salt serum instead of vitamins and probably took X-rays with the help of a vacuum cleaner. Then he went home to his vineyards and orange groves to drink brandy and listen to Beethoven.'

'My mother was scared to go to the modern hospital.' My voice is too soft.

Doctor P eats the breadcrumbs in his hand. 'She was right. Why should the colonial doctor be any better than the colonial policeman?'

I wind my hair round my finger and Rabah watches me curiously. 'The body must feel it has something worthwhile to get well for,' the doctor says, smiling at me. 'Would you be so kind as to take this hatbox to number six for me?'

*

Yes.

When I return Ahmed says, 'Congratulations, Yasmina the Avenger. You have carried pamphlets in that hatbox to our head-quarters.'

The doctor smiles at me again. 'So you are an Avenger?'

'Yes,' I whisper.

He thinks for a while. 'Those pamphlets you carried in the hat-box are not to be worn on the head, but in the head. So it is true to say you have been carrying headware.' He turns to Ahmed.

'What is the name of the woman who printed them on my duplicator?'

'Safia.'

'Why do you ask?'

'Because the room smells of absinthe when she leaves.' The doctor turns his attention to Ahmed. 'Your throat is sore because you smoke cigarette butts. You'd be better off smoking your shoes.'

Ahmed the jackal, with his hard face and fists, shrugs.

'I'm okay.'

'Our *pied-noir* comrade,' Rabah says to me, 'has just finished operating on one of our leaders shot in the abdomen.' The doctor says nothing.

'Where do you live in France?' I do not want to talk about death. He shuts his eyes and says in a bored voice, 'Marseille, Lyon. Lille. My hair used to be straight when I lived in France. Since I've been here it's gone curly.' He glances at me and then says to Rabah, 'I miss good cheese.'

'Does Brie make your hair curly?'

'I am telling you now, Rabah,' the doctor smothers his smile, 'the French authorities are going to put an embargo on anti-tetanus vaccine. No Algerian will be able to get hold of the stuff. You must think about this now.' The smile suddenly appears again. 'You know what? I am tired already. And the war has only just started.'

'The war has not just started.' Ahmed takes a butt out of his pocket, rolls it between his fingers and lights up. 'Where there are *colons* there is always war.'

'Rabah,' Doctor P's voice is without emotion, 'your comrade died before I operated. He had a hole in his intestine from gunshot. One of his colleagues must have given him water when he asked for it. If someone has a wound in the stomach they must not on any account be given water.' Rabah nods, his shoulders shrunk with pain. He leaves the room.

'Yasmina,' the doctor is talking to me again.

'Yes.'

'I would like you to tell me one day about your brother.'

'Why?'

'You'll sleep better after.'

Rabah must have told him how I am afraid to sleep. If I shut my eyes everyone will be dead when I wake up.

'Why are you called Doctor P?'

'Because I am paranoid,' he says.

I can feel love, like a force, pushing itself into my body.

13

The American is pushing himself into my body and he is saying, Oh baby. Leaning on his elbows, blue eyes half-closed. Baby baby baby. He turns his head towards the doorway and groans.

I shut my eyes so that I need not see the blue eye of Jane who is peering round the corner of the door, waiting for the man who has bought me to notice her.

14

Ahmed does not want to be noticed. He lurks around corners, unseen, plotting. Sometimes I go out with him on to the streets where he cleans shoes. His fingers are always black from the polish and he sucks them all day long. 'Stops my hunger pains,' he scowls at the sun. Sometimes he tells me about his love affairs. They are always short because he has to change address so often. Ahmed is a fugitive in his own city, moving from one hideout to another, just as he moves from one shoe to another, spitting and polishing, holding out his hand for coins, a brown cap pushed over his eyes.

'The F.L.N. is like the small pox.' He unwraps a bar of chocolate stolen from a vendor and stuffs it into his mouth. 'It will spread across the body of Algiers.'

Every morning Safia, who is Ahmed's best friend, teaches him how to read and write in Rabah's apartment. His first words are a note to her. 'QUIT SMOKING.' She punches him in the stomach.

'I do what I like.'

'I learn to write and get punched,' he says.

Safia distracts him by writing him a note. 'WHAT ARE YOUR PRINCIPAL TARGETS?' He reads the words, sucking his fingers, and slowly begins to write, changing letters, crossing words out.

'My principal targets are: 1. Radio stations. 2. The telephone exchange. 3. The gasworks.'

Rabah interrupts us. He carries a small leather suitcase and he is in his best suit.

'Goodbye.'

Rabah always has a suitcase in his hand. I want to go with him when he leaves, but he just shakes his head and says, 'Tough.'

'Where are you going?'

'Tunisia.' Ahmed and Safia seem to already know this. I am always the last to know everything.

'Who is she?'

Rabah laughs. 'It's like living with a jealous wife.' He kisses my head. 'She is politics,' he says, taking money from his wallet and giving it to me. I am scared he will not come back. Everyone we know is in gaol. The French regularly round up innocent suspects and send them to prison.

Safia says she knows of mild family men who want an easy life. They want to eat their food and play with their children. Instead they are turned into ardent militants in prison. Marx and Lenin are smuggled into the gaols.

Doctor P breaks a loaf of bread into three pieces and puts it on the table with a plate of cheeses. 'Help yourself.'

I try the cheese but it is not to my taste. He smiles at me and clasps his small hands behind his head.

'I don't know what else to give you. Perhaps some soup?'

I shake my head.

'You will like the soup,' he encourages me. 'I made it last night. Beans and tomato.'

I break a piece of bread and chew it slowly.

'What are you thinking about, Yasmina?'

'I love you,' I say.

Doctor P pours himself a small glass of red wine.

'Talk to me about Omar.'

'Omar was my brother. The gendarmes cut him. Here.' I point to my crotch.

He nods.

'They cut him and he bled.'

He nods again.

'And then I ran away.'

'That must have made you frightened for a long time,' he says.

'I love you,' I say again.

He thinks for a while, and then lifts up his head and smiles at me. 'Thank you.' His voice is quiet.

'When you can't sleep what do you think about?'

'Nothing.'

'What does nothing look like?'

I get up from the table and walk to him. He sits very still, playing with the cheese on his plate. When I put my arms around his neck and press my lips to his cheek, he pulls me off him.

'Tell me about Omar.'

Now I am weeping, and he is sitting opposite me, drinking wine.

'There's a lot to cry about,' he says. I cry more because that morning I had coiled up my hair in a new style, two hours in front of the mirror sculpting and fiddling with pins and water. For him, who does not love me. I watched my new face, turning my head this way and that way, and I put kohl on my eyes, and looked again and looked again and then turned away in shame and excitement at the spectre of my small beauty staring back at me.

15

'You fucking bastard.' Jane stands over the bed, hands in her trouser pockets, tapping her sandalled feet.

'Where is Jim right now, Jack?'

The American has put the sheet over his head.

'I'll tell you where he is. I go buy bread and vegetables for the kids. Pick them up from the minder. Cook for them. See this stuff on my shirt? Where it's wet around my breasts? That's milk. That's the stuff I feed Jim's baby with. I put them down to sleep. Tell them stories. Swipe at the flies that settle on them like shit. Tell them they're going to be okay when they cry, persuade them not to be scared, get into bed with them and hold them and try and answer their fucking questions. Is there a God? Will He make us die? You're going to be fine, Nancy, you're not going to die. Where's Dad? Dad's coming back soon. I get them listening to the birds in the trees. I get them to sleep. And then I go find their father. Someone gives me this rat-dive address. I walk there in a daze. I walk there worried my kids are gonna wake up. I walk there in a damp shirt. I get lost and have to ask directions. Turn right here, you'll come to a blue wall, take a left, no not at the blue wall, at the fountain. Do I need this kind of grief? And then when I find him, where is he?'

She kicks the bed.

'He's fucking a whore.'

Silence.

'I'm at home putting band-aids on his daughter's knee where she fell over and grazed herself and I'm going crazy because I can't read or write or think or put cream on my face because every-where I look there's a kid bawlin' for me.

She folds her arms across her shirt and circles the room.

'In my twenties, y' know, there is no way I'm gonna die in some suburb eating cocktail sausages on sticks. Drinking dry martinis and showing folks my new floorpolisher and power mower. I'm not going to host Sunday barbecues on the lawn and clean the station wagon while my kids are at cub scouts.' She opens the glass doors, walks outside and stares at the sea.

When she comes back in again, the room fills with her perfume.

The American is still hiding under the white sheet pretending to be dead.

'The grown men I drank beer with all wanted girl wives to make them omelettes in their underwear and take phone messages and give them babies. Even though they said stuff like "pad" and "bread" and they "dug" shit, they still wanted women to look after them, just like their mothers looked after their fathers, and to always be sexy and admiring and to never give him a hard time EVER with her own fucking nightmares and whateverthefuck she needed to convince herself to hang in there. You've gotta make yourself stupid for love, isn't that right, sweet heart?'

Silence.

'And then I'm thinking, well Janey, how's the time for big love. Get it together. I am a beautiful woman in a man's world. And as it happens, its not that much fun. I mean what must it be like to be a beautiful man in a man's world?'

Silence.

'So I meet Jim. Bring me home, Jim Boy. We go travelling and it's wild. Y'know, Jacko, in Mexico there was this armadillo that would only sleep in my hair! If the armadillo wasn't awake Jim knew I was still asleep. We spent our time reading and talking and riding horses. Jim, who I love above all others, respect and want for all time as you know, Time is Jim's science thing. He's making mathematics out of the future and the past. He's happy in the present, taking the armadillo out of my hair, squeezing oranges and sewing the loose buckle of his sandals back on with a needle and thread.'

'Trouble is, back home, we can't make a home. This is New York. Jim says, give up your room, Janey, come and live with me. I live with him for a year with my life packed in boxes, stacked in his cellar. I write on a rickety table he bought for five dollars some place – total junk – and he's writing on a desk with anglepoise lamps and filing cabinets, with his life all organized – but it doesn't matter. Why? 'Cause, well, we meet at six o'clock for cocktails. He made great margaritas in those days, Jack. Remember? He taught me how to make them too, a mean ol' mother with lots of lime. We were a citrus family. Sometimes there wasn't anything in the house except bowls of lemons and limes. We cooked cheap good food. Saw movies, browsed bookshops. Until, Jacko, it dawns on this mad broad . . .'

She shakes him.

'That I am being ripped off! So this was the man I was going to spend my life with? We talked about it. How we would have a quality life and not reduce each other, not become one of those couples you see who sit in restaurants not talking to each other except to review the food: you like the trout, Eddie? Yeah it's okay, how's your steak? In our lovetalk we made gardens and studies and chutneys and marvelled at all the books we had not read. We would have a garden full of cacti. Like we saw in Mexico. And wild roses with those big muckerfucking thorns. What did we want? I wanted to write novels and Jim, being the humble man he is, wanted to rewrite the laws of the universe. We wanted to make babies and laze around in this garden we sketched out for each other. Cats and salads and glasses of wine, playing with our beautiful kids, watering our rose bushes, reading newspapers and smiling at the wonder of it all. Thing is Jacko – you with me?'

'I'm with you, Jane.'

'Thing is, we would talk about this stuff but he was happy with me living half a life, despite all the fancy talk about a whole life. It was just talk. My belongings in his cellar and all. It suited him well. His head was in space most of the time. The joke is, his kind of science, it's all about interconnectedness. A unified way of thinking about nature, how human beings behave, co-evolution and structure. He's fine with galaxies and planets, he's fine checking out artificial life, but when it comes to our life, he says, slow down, don't get real, babe, just relax.'

She stops because the door opens and Jim walks in with Safia following behind him.

'I love you, Janey,' Jim says.

'Cocksucker.'

Backlit like a vengeful angel, the beacon flashing across her blonde rage, she stares at Safia's short black hair. Jim's eyes have become empty. He fixes vacantly on the door. Safia leans against the wall in her cream kaftan and smokes a cigarette.

Jack peers over the sheet, and grins.

'Hi,' he says to Jim and then cocks his head at Safia. 'Hey, have you got a cigarette?'

'Pay me for it,' she replies.

'Shit!' He shakes his head, searching on the floor for his cigarette packet. 'I don't pay for a drag on some butt.'

'Yeah, shit.' Safia draws heavily on her cigarette.

Jane walks over to the table by the bed, picks up the pistol and points it at her husband's head.

'Hi, Jim,' she says.

'What do you want, Jane?'

'I want you to sing for your supper, Jim. Startin' now.'

16

Safia's belly is swollen. There is a hectic flush to her cheeks. 'I feel sick,' she whimpers. 'My breasts have turned blue. I rub salt on the nipples in seven circles so as to protect my milk. My back hurts. I get cravings for kif and honey and coral and silver. My stomach is so mighty, I think it's twins. But my black hair shines, yes?'

'Yes,' I reply. Her hair is sleek and lustrous. 'Why do you keep it short, Safia?'

'So I can see,' she says in a matter-of-fact voice.

'Yasmina, I can feel her move. She's hard, my daughter. Got no curves. All sharp edges and cold skin. I'm eating for millions, you know. My appetite is rampant. Know what she likes? Not prunes. Not stew. Not couscous with salted butter. Want to feel her?'

I put my hands on her belly. It is bulky and sharp, like she says it is.

She opens her haik to reveal a web of string and straps tied to her body. Tucked under them are a mass of automatic pistols, gun clips and grenades.

'Now I have to travel all the way to Kabylia,' she sighs.

'Why don't you put them in a suitcase?'

'What do you think? The patrols will open and examine its contents,' she snaps, irritated, rearranging the folds of her haik.

'My niece. She is seven years old. A French soldier burnt her arm. Just for the hell of it.' Safia walks like a beast of burden around Rabah's apartment.

'Oh the weight of it. It's very heavy this stuff, you know.' She rubs her back. 'The most important thing is to give the impression that my hands are free, then I will not be stopped. This look okay?' She holds up her hands.

I nod.

'Do these hands look humble and servile enough for you?'

'No.'

She makes the wrists go limp. 'Better?'

'Much better.' I put some of Rabah's dates in her hand. 'Is Ahmed waiting for you?'

'You look. He should be outside.' She devours the dates hungrily. 'Rabah has fine tastes. Perhaps you have some almonds for me to eat on the bus?'

I do not answer her because I am looking out of the window. Ahmed is polishing the grocer's shoes on the pavement outside the apartment, but something else is happening. An old woman is pressed against the wall, her hands above her head, while a patrol runs something over her body. It looks like a frying pan.

She is frozen, a black rock, while the young man examines her. Now he waves her on, but her arms are still stuck above her head.

He shouts something at her and she slowly comes to life and begins to walk, but her arms have not come down yet, as if it is painful for her to move her bones. When I tell Safia she just shrugs. 'That's normal. The frying pan is a magnetic detector for weapons.'

'You can't go out there.' These days I am frightened all the time. My guts ache with fear and there is no one to tell.

'If he puts that thing over your body you're finished.'

She finishes chewing her dates. 'Is Ahmed there?'

'Yes.'

'It's okay.' She smiles, showing her two rotten front teeth. 'I will walk ahead of Ahmed. He'll follow me. If anything happens to me he will intervene.'

'Take the dates with you.' I give her the lot. Never one to be polite, she does not refuse and she does not thank me.

Goodbye. Rabah is always saying goodbye. He can say goodbye in twelve languages. I am sixteen years of age.

Goodbye.

This morning he carries the same old suitcase, coat slung over his arm, dabbing perfume on his brow and the back of his neck with a yellow silk handkerchief.

'A little orange in this rose,' he says, taking off his Egyptian watch.

'For you.' He hands it to me.

'Thanks.' I am always gloomy when Rabah says goodbye.

'Yasmina, you are an angry girl. Why is that, huh?' He straps the watch on to my wrist and, when it doesn't fit, he makes a new hole for the buckle.

'There. Perfect.'

'What are you doing in Paris?'

'Ah.' His voice is stern. 'That is why I never had children. Because I would have had to leave too often. It is politics that separate us.'

'You do what you want to do. That's all.' I turn my back on him. He sighs.

'Goodbye.'

We are both silent. 'Goodbye,' he says again.

'Goodbye.'

He picks up his suitcase and slams the door.

'I love you darkly.'

That is what my mother said to me in a dream. She runs towards me, excited, shouting, 'I want to die.' Knowing she wants me to say, please don't die I want you to live, I reply 'Die then, that's a good idea. I won't be sorry.' Whereupon she falls on the floor and rolls her eyes towards me and fakes her own death. 'You are the most important thing in the whole wide world,' she cries to me, but her voice is mocking. 'You are the centre of my universe. I love you darkly.' I want to kiss her but feel queasy. 'Of course everything I've just said is rubbish!' she howls with laughter, clutching her sides and rolling on the floor.

I tell this to Doctor P. When I say the words I love you darkly I feel like a fool. So I laugh. What's so funny, he asks me? I don't want to cry. Ever again. I want to laugh and smoke kif with Safia and eat ice-cream. 'I am no good for you,' Doctor P says lightly. 'I am not a curer of souls. I might as well be called Doctor Paralysis or Doctor Paradox. A doctor is just a dictionary. He gives a name to symptoms the patient does not know the meaning of. You ask me to explain feelings you do not know the meaning of. But who am I? All I can say is yes that is yellow fever. That is malaria. Sometimes I go to the campsite and sleep under the stars in the Sahara. I send home a carpet from Ghardaïa or buy souvenirs for my family from Touareg or el Oued. When I go to Tunis I look at mosaics. Sometimes I buy halva and pretzel sticks and watch the ferries from Europe arrive at the port. There is little to do except try to give to each other maximum dignity. But I am a fool. It is you who will have to give me back my dignity. Where Safia is now will be decimated by French napalm bombs. It's a shame, I like the forests there. Does she look after you while Rabah is away?'

'Yes.'

'If you told your uncle you are frightened, he wouldn't go away so much,' he says, standing up.

When Safia arrives from Kabylia, one week later, she is no longer a mother-to-be. 'I've dropped my babies,' she says. 'They've been adopted. Don't think I'm heartless, I made sure they went to good homes.' She yawns, drinking a can of milk, her long legs stretched out on the floor. 'In Kabylia the cedars are blue. White doves slept on my face.' She tells me this while we laze on cushions in the heat of the afternoon. 'Kabylia is paradise. It has many caves and that is good.'

'Why?'

'Caves are good for guerillas,' she says. 'They can disappear.'

'I am frightened,' I say.

'In Kabylia,' she continues, ignoring me, 'there are caves and there are fig trees. I know five families who own one fig tree between them. I like to spend whole days lazing under that tree. Yes, I like to stretch my mind under its leaves and think about melting into holes in the hills.

'I spent a lot of time under that fig tree. I reckon we stole nine hundred farms and four hundred agricultural machines back from the French in all that lazing I do.' She lights another cigarette. 'Our leaders have banned cigarettes,' she says in a mock-complaining voice. 'If they catch me smoking they will cut off my nose.'

'Why?'

'We don't want to put money in the pockets of *pied-noir* vine and tobacco growers, do we? I used to have to smoke at the back of the pastry shop when I was at the university.' She stands up and walks in circles around the carpets.

'What's this, Yasmina?'

'What?'

'The French making a study of guerilla techniques. They think we walk in circles to pass time.'

'Rabah should have been home three days ago.'

'So what?' Safia says scornfully. 'What's your problem? This is not a party, you know. This is a war.'

'Three days is a long time.'

I don't know where Safia comes from or where she sleeps at night. Sometimes I see her with another woman at the market selling grain and she pretends not to have seen me. Safia is clever, but she also frightens me. She sleeps with doves while organising country folk in total warfare against the French. Her kaftan is stained with saffron. I do not know her age. Her green eyes sometimes turn to glass and she falls asleep on her feet.

'Tell me where Rabah is.'

'I don't know!' she shouts back.

'You're no good, Safia.'

'Is that so?'

'Have you got a mother?'

'What do you think, Yasmina? I hatched out of a snake-egg?'

'Rabah should have been home by now,' I say again.

'Rabah takes his own time.'

'He's got responsibilities.'

'Like what, Yasmina?'

'Me!' I bang my fist into my chest.

Safia strokes my bare feet lazily with her long brown fingers, the gold and turquoise rings she wears cold on my flesh. I often sleep with my head in the lap of her peppermint kaftan, and she half sleeps too, sucking the sugar cubes I put in my tea. When the door bangs twice, she says, 'It is Ahmed. Open the door.'

'He's got a key, you know he has.'

Safia's fingers stroke my hair and cheek, her rough voice cursing flies that come too near.

My mother rolls on the floor, clutching her sides and howling with laughter. 'Here's your breakfast,' she screams. 'Now grow! Here's your lunch. Grow! Here's an orange. Grow!'

'Where's my father?' I wail at her. 'Every daughter always

wants to know where her father is.' She slaps her thighs. 'But I don't know. I don't know. He's gone. Lost. Slipped away. Not here. Gone. Gone. Gone.'

'Yasmina, hey Yasmina, wake up.'

'Rabah?'

Ahmed is whispering to Safia like he always does, telling her not to drink and smoke, or she telling him where she has been, how many leaflets she has printed and how many weapons she has hauled in. Ahmed has his mouth close to her ear, while Safia listens, deadpan, shaking her sleek black head. She stands up and walks to the sink where she soaks a cloth of cold water and runs it over her hair.

'Give me a cigarette.' Ahmed points to her tobacco.

'You don't smoke.'

'That's right,' he says. 'I don't.' And lights up.

'You've got a new tattoo.' I point to the three black dots on his wrist.

'Know what it means?'

'What?'

'It means, My Crazy Life.'

'Get on with it, Ahmed.' Safia is smoking kif.

'Get on with what?' I ask, straight into Ahmed's tense face.

'Rabah is dead,' he says, looking ahead of him at the wall.

'Yes,' I reply. And watch the tips of their cigarettes glow.

*

Yes.

There are tears in Ahmed's eyes, but not in mine. They spill down his face while he smokes. Safia puts the cloth over her head again. Someone else is knocking on the door. Safia lets in Doctor P. He carries Rabah's suitcase in his hand, drops it on the carpet and sits down.

'Yasmina?'

What does he want me to say, this stupid French man? Hello, I am very well, thank you? Ahmed is weeping with his back to me and I am coldly, mathematically, counting my losses. It is simple addition. My father, my brother, my mother, my uncle. Wiped out. Nothing there. Lost. Slipped away. Gone. Gone. Gone. Yet the room is full. Two street hoods and a doctor called Paranoid.

'Go away,' I say to them all. 'I live here, not you.'

'She's in shock.' Doctor P frowns.

'We don't need a doctor to tell us what we feel,' Safia snarls at him. 'We know what we feel.'

They are like statues, all of them, sitting, standing, leaning. Ahmed is a fountain. Water keeps spurting from him. The smoke from Safia's kif wafts through the room. The doctor loosens his white collar. Ahmed turns towards us.

'I'm going to tell you how he died,' he says to me.

Safia flexes her ankle, turning it in circles, round and round. Ahmed speaks with no emotion, softly and very fast.

'Rabah was arrested on his way back from Paris. Someone had information about him and gave it to the police. He carried money collected for the revolution from France in his suitcase. He also had notebooks for two articles he was writing about how whites in Toulouse are gunning us down on the street. When he would not talk, they stripped him naked. They pumped his stomach full of water and put electric shocks through his body. First in his mouth. The spasms made his heart race and he had a heart attack. So they left him and then they came back. On the third day when he would not speak, they thought it was because his tongue had swollen from the electrodes. So they gave him another break. In the break young French officers and soldiers talked to him and he spoke. Rabah said to them, you must stop this, you are injuring your-selves. It is one of the officers who gave me this information. They said to Rabah, we know that the man who places the bomb is just an arm. Tomorrow it will be replaced by another arm. But tell us the names of the men the arms belong to. We must understand their brain. You can help us understand. When Rabah would not speak they hung him from his thumbs. That was the end of Rabah.'

Yes.

I walk over to the suitcase. 'I told you to leave my house.'

'They called me in to examine his body,' Doctor P says, stand-ing up.

'I thought you might want the suitcase. Now I must get back to work. Coughs, colds, headaches, stomach aches.' He pauses.

'You know where I live.'

'I hate you,' I say.

Safia looks at Ahmed, who makes a gesture like swatting a fly with his hand, and then gently touches the doctor's shoulder.

'All the same, you know where I live.' His face is pale.

'I hate you,' I say again. He puts his hands in his pockets and leaves. Ahmed plays with his tattoo. My Crazy Life. Algiers. 1957.

'On Sunday,' Ahmed says softly, 'you will carry a bomb into the heart of European Algiers.'

Ahmed looks younger. He looks like a young boy. Perhaps that is why he takes sunglasses out of his pocket and puts them over his eyes.

'At home, I have two loaves of bread, seven oranges, a small piece of lamb, one jar of honey, seventy kilos of explosive, two thousand mercury detonators, three hundred electric detonators, five beds for my chemistry students to sleep in and a pair of pyjamas for myself.'

'See you on Sunday,' I say.

Safia sleeps with me that night. At dawn I walk out of bed and open Rabah's suitcase in the half-light. There are only two objects in the case. The police must have removed everything else. The silk handkerchief. And a book. It is not philosophy. It is not poetry. It is a tourist guide to Paris. Something is stuck between the pages. Two tickets, in the section titled Dance Halls – *bals musettes. Afternoon tangos to fill the afternoon hours. Come and tango at Balajo on the rue de Lappe. Métro Bastille. Waltz, tango, java, cha-cha.*

The roads are beginning to fill with early morning traffic. Car horns and birds. Often at this time Rabah would be typing in his room. I would hear the tap of the keys and make him coffee, or he would make me coffee. That is how he knew I could not sleep because I myself am tortured every night. I am tortured in my sleep. Nightmares that wake me, shivering, scared of the pictures I have seen and the dream information received. My uncle, unshaven in his slippers, half-parent, half-companion. My most loved man. My most loved everything. When he shouted at me I shouted back, and when he said goodbye, I said, goodbye.

17

'I said sing for your supper.'

Jane takes a step backwards, lifts up the pistol and shoots at the ceiling. Plaster falls on to the concrete floor.

Safia takes out a piece of chewing gum and lazily puts it into her mouth.

'Janey,' Jack pleads with her. 'Put that damn weapon down.'

'Is that what you want?' She shoots at his boot lying by the bed. It jumps into the air and breaks into three pieces. Safia, still chewing, says, 'If you're going to use that gun, aim right.' She points to me, 'You touch her and I'll cut your throat.'

Jane smiles. 'Yeah? Is that a promise? Should have come looking for you earlier. I need someone to finish me off.' She slides her hand into the pocket of her slacks and takes out three white chalky pills. 'Codeine.' She throws them into her mouth and chews slowly. 'It's a good anaesthetic but I figure I'd still feel the knife. Better to blow me away with this.' She waves the pistol at Safia. 'Put me out of my misery then, lady.'

Safia starts to walk towards the gun, but Jim stops her. It takes a lot to stop Safia once she has set her mind on something. Safia is indestructible.

'These are my love words, Janey.'

Jane is looking straight at him, but she is somewhere else too, chewing the codeine. Safia walks back to the wall, blinking the sun away from her long green eyes.

'Nothing in the world can hurt me as much as you can, Jane. Honey. I'm stone in love with you. My happiest thing, Jane, is you. My precious. My true love. You are everything. You and me and our kids and all we have made together is everything. There isn't anything more important to me than that.'

Jane holds the pistol firm in her fingers.

'I want to make myself plain to you,' she says. 'We must say the things we want. I want to give you all that I am. I may look like a princess but there's a toad inside me. I'll tell you what everything is. That's me holding this pistol right here. I want to murder you. That's everything.'

Jane smiles at Safia, who looks down at her plastic sandals, arms folded across her chest.

'What do you think I should cook the kids for supper tonight?'

*

She sighs, her hands tense on the gun. 'What are you here for, Jack 'n' Jim? The carpets? The climate? The magic? The souks? The sleepy camels way down on the beach? You here for the drugs? Cat got your tongue, Jim?'

'I'm a stranger everywhere, Janey. But I don't want to be a stranger to you. I don't want us to fall apart. I can't talk to you with a godamn gun in your hand. Let's leave this place and sort ourselves out.'

'Stay right where you are.' She clicks the gun and aims it at his crotch, all the time speaking over her shoulder to Jack.

'How about you, Jack, what you here for? To broaden your mind or something? Is that it? What words do you speak in cafés? Do you say *adios* or *au revoir*? I kinda feel better with *adios*. What words do you know in Spanish? *Pasteleria. Perfumeria. Banco. Menu del dia.* It makes me sick. I want to chuck my life up into some piss bucket. Myself, I like the palms and the sad creaking they do at night when I lie awake.'

Her blue eyes burn black, hair the colour of ash. Jim looks at Jack and runs his fingers across his forehead. She continues.

'Last night, someone took me out to eat this thing, um, a little pigeon in puff pastry. I puked in the toilet. Not because it wasn't good because it was . . .' She stops. This time she looks Jim in the eye. 'Because I am so damn sad I won't be happy till I've blown you to bits.'

'Janey.' Jack climbs out of bed and starts to put his jeans on.

'Let's go have a coffee and talk.'

'Get the fuck out of my way.'

'I want to talk to you, Janey.'

'Which Janey do you want to talk to, Jack?'

'You.'

She shakes her head. 'Take those jeans off and get back into that bed with your little Janey over there . . .' Her eyes are hard, pearly fingernail pointing at me. Hair falling over her face, she slips off her sandals so she can grip the floor better.

'I said, take those jeans off!'

Jack is nervous. 'Okay, okay.' He slides the jeans down his hips.

'Go on, Jack. I want you to talk to Jane.'

'I'm ready for you, babe.' He grins at her.

'Talk to her.' She waves her hand towards me.

His big body freezes under the sheet. Two red patches creep into his cheeks.

'She doesn't speak English,' he mumbles, running his nicotine-yellow fingers over the stubble on his jaw.

'Yes, she does,' Safia says.

'You heard the lady,' Jane shouts. 'C'mon.'

The American lies on his back staring at the plaster falling off the ceiling. Every time a new piece falls he shudders.

'How did you get those scars on your body, darlin'?' he whispers, still staring at the ceiling.

'Can't hear you!' Safia shouts.

'How did you get those marks on your body?'

'A French soldier put wires around my stomach and cut me.' When I find my voice it is matter-of-fact. I also stare at the ceiling.

Jack blows through his teeth.

'Um, why did he do that to you?'

'I bombed a café in Algiers.'

Jack clears his throat. 'Enough conversation for you, Janey?'

'You only just started, Jacko.'

He tries to laugh, looking at Jim, who shakes his head and then cradles his forehead with its stripe of sunburn in his big hands.

'What? You just felt like um . . . it's Monday, bombing day today?'

'They killed my uncle.'

'Right.' The American looks at the ceiling again. 'How'd he catch you, this French soldier?'

'A doctor working for the police knew where I was staying. They came to get me.'

'I don't suppose they gave you milk and cookies.'

'They put wires around my stomach and cut me.'

'Yeah.' He presses his cheek into the starched white pillow and closes his eyes.

'What about your mom and pop? Did they come and get you?'

'They are dead.'

'It's just been one big car crash for you, hasn't it, darlin'?'

18

'Look.' Ahmed takes off his socks.

The words Shut Up are tattooed in black dye on the sole of his right foot. 'Anyone shouts at me, I show them my foot.' He walks to a small box piled with stolen chocolate and breaks a bar into three pieces. 'My Crazy Life. Shut Up. That is me me me, Ahmed the jackal,' he hisses at Safia when she refuses her share of chocolate.

'Not strong enough to get you high, eh?'

Safia is nervous today. But not Ahmed. 'I got the chocolate for you,' he turns on her, hurt.

The casbah is his city. He walks us through walls. Behind each wall is another wall. I am lost in his labyrinth, eating chocolate in one of the rooms of the hideout. He has been preparing for this day, Sunday, and I am waiting for his orders. When the French blew up a house full of women and children thinking it was a bomb factory, Ahmed's people waited for his signal and then shot down fifty civilians. Everywhere we go we are under curfew and we are searched.

My Crazy Life. Shut Up.

Ahmed tells us for the fifth time that this afternoon we will give European Algiers a heart attack. He calls it the Heart Quake.

'I am going to wash your hair.'

Safia heats up water and stands behind me, mixing a paste that makes my eyes water.

'What is it?'

'Ammonia.'

She combs it through my hair. 'Now we must wait an hour. You are going to be a superblonde.' I laugh. Perhaps I will look like Rabah's American. I imagine her to be like Marilyn Monroe, curled up on a rug in a polka dot dress, laughing at Rabah's jokes.

'I don't like blondes,' Safia murmurs.

'You are nervous,' I reply.

Ahmed comes back into the room, carrying something under his arm. It is a bright summer dress, sleeveless, with big white cotton daisies embroidered on to the cotton.

'Where did you get it?'

'Safia stole it from the daughter of the woman she cleans for.'

'Why do you clean houses when you went to the university?' I do not understand Safia.

She feels my wet sticky hair with her fingers.

'That's how it is at the moment.'

'She teaches us how to read and write,' Ahmed says, and I can see he is proud of her, despite their fights.

'And what does he write?' Safia shakes her head at me, pointing at Ahmed.

'My Crazy Life. Shut Up!' he shouts.

She smiles.

'You will look like a *pied-noir* girl going to the beach.' Ahmed turns away while I put the dress on. Safia zips me up, smoothing the cotton over my hips.

'Your name is Denise,' she says, her deadpan face pale in the dark room.

'Denise,' I repeat.

I remember the girls I saw dancing on the beaches when I was five years old on Rabah's lap. I know them better than they know themselves. Safia is anxious that I will not be able to move freely in the dress, so I swing my hips for her. Ahmed laughs at me, biting his black nails, encouraging me, yelping, 'Eh, Yasmina!' his face serious, thinking something through. He asks me to practise walking and running. My eyes are watering from the ammonia in my hair as I run down the corridors, tears spilling out of me. The more they come the more I skip and run and jump and swirl my hips, but they keep on coming and I keep on moving until my head feels strange. I am falling. Safia puts her hand on my arm and I bite her hand to stop the pain in my head. She stays right there with me, my teeth marks in her hand, she doesn't move it from my mouth, she stands still and waits.

Rabah Rabah Rabah.

'Come on then.' Safia pulls me to her, and starts to wash the paste off my hair.

Who am I now?

I am ginger. Black eyebrows and ginger hair. It is not Marilyn Monroe who stares back at me in the mirror, but a hybrid woman, not this and not that. Similar to the *pieds-noirs* who are neither French nor Algerian. Zohra, Ahmed's girlfriend, walks in and laughs when she sees me. She sweeps my bleached hair into a pony-tail while Safia paints my lips and fingernails red. Safia's black hair is hidden underneath a straw hat. Today she wears a white kaftan and white sandals.

'You can't wear this,' she says pointing to Rabah's Egyptian watch on my wrist. A man's watch, heavy gold and thick black strap. 'Take it off.'

'I want to wear it.' My voice sounds strange and she remains quiet.

Ahmed shakes his head. 'Take it off.'

Safia sips her absinthe.

'No.' I shake my bleached mad head.

Ahmed has stopped smiling. He is quiet and he is solemn. His voice makes us calm. He has prepared a beach bag for me. Inside it is a bikini, a towel and suntan lotion. 'Feel the weight,' he says to Safia. She takes it from him and nods. 'The bomb weighs little more than a kilogramme.' Ahmed is pleased.

'Where is it?'

'Wrapped inside the towel.' He gives me a forged identity card.

'Denise,' I say.

'If you are stopped by a Zouave, you say you are going to the beach.'

My target is a café popular with *pieds-noirs* and European students on their way home from the beach.

'Remember,' Ahmed says, 'if you lose your nerve, there is no difference between the girl who places a bomb in the European café, and the man who strapped electrodes on to the body of Rabah.' He shakes my hand and I am surprised it is damp. He is more nervous than I am. I look at Safia and Zohra. They smile at me. Zohra at the last minute ties a white ribbon round my ponytail. Ahmed carefully puts the bag over my shoulder.

'Walk for us.'

I walk for them, light-hearted and brisk. They clap and cheer.

'A little more lip-paint,' Zohra whispers.

Safia puts more colour on my lips and, as an after-thought, takes a black pencil and makes a beauty spot under my eye.

'Yasmina,' she says softly, 'when you go into the café order a cola first. Drink it and then leave your bag under the table, okay?'

'Okay.'

'Don't talk to anyone in the café.' Ahmed's eyes are too bright. I can smell sweat and cigarette smoke.

'Make yourself calm here.' Zohra touches a place on my stomach.

I nod at them all, their faces pulled with nerves into stupid smiles. Zohra clears up the ammonia paste.

The sun is shining. It is a lazy Sunday afternoon and I walk cheerfully, the bag swinging on my shoulder. When an old woman smiles at my youth and vigour, I smile back. A man sitting on the bench under a tree also looks up at me. Who cares? I am a made-up person. I can do what I like. Bleached hair, beauty spot and painted fingernails. I am three hours old. How to speak? How to walk? How to think? Where to look with my three-hour eyes? In my three-hour life the sun is shining, it is Sunday, no one has died, no one has disappeared, no one has been tortured, an old woman has smiled at me, a man has admired me, I am more than ready for my glorious new life.

'Hey!'

Almost immediately I am stopped by a Zouave. I smile him a three-hour smile and he smiles back. He is apologetic when he asks for my identity card. I search for it in my bag but he hardly looks at it when I give it to him.

'Where are you going?'

To Saint-Eugène beach. 'Perhaps I can come with you?'

'Sure,' I reply and flick my ginger pony-tail.

'Another time, hey? I'm on duty now.' Okay. He gives me back the card, holding my three-hour hand for too long.

I walk away. But he stands there watching me. Why doesn't he go away?'

'Hey!' he calls again.

'Oui?' I glance over my shoulder.

'What's your name?' Denise. I shout my three-hour name and wave. I know I must keep walking but he won't let me go.

'Denise.' He runs back to me. 'I forgot to search your bag.' Now I am sweating. 'Look,' I say, 'I told you I'm going to the beach.' I hold the bag open. My bikini. My towel, some magazines. 'Show me your bikini,' he leers at me. 'Haven't you seen a bikini before?' I put my hands on my hips. 'But I want to see yours.'

'Since when do I have to show my bikini to the police?'

'Okay,' he shrugs. 'Have a good swim. Shame I can't come with you.'

I walk away too fast.

Outside the café I can hear the jukebox. Couples inside are dancing to the mambo. I watch them for a while through the glass panes and then walk in. The white cotton daisies tremble across my stomach. Mothers and their children sip milkshakes. I order a cola and pay, find a seat by the window and look out. The women are making their way to the cinema and the men to their yacht club. Someone turns up the volume of the mambo and more people get up to dance. I get up too. But not to dance. I leave my bag under the table, my mouth still full of cola, and try to weave my way through the dancing bodies. A young man calls out to me. Do I want to dance? No. I must swallow the cola in my mouth but I don't know how to. I'm caught between their tanned legs and arms as the mambo changes and the girls scream 'Elvis!' A wopbopaloobop – alopbamboom! Their pony-tails like mine, flicking up and down, hand-jiving, shaking their hips and flirting with boys. 'Kiss me, baby!' a boy shouts to me. 'Tomorrow!' I shout back, cola spilling down my dress.

Tutti-frutti! All rootie!

When I turn up an alleyway I hear the explosion. Glass shattering. My eyes shut, and still the glass is falling.

*

Shut Up, My Crazy Life. 1957.

I open my eyes because there is a stabbing pain in my stomach. Something is pressing into the cotton of my daisy dress and someone has locked my shoulders because I cannot move, their hot breath too near my face. A gendarme is poking his baton into my stomach, pushing me backwards towards the wall, all the time saying, I saw you running, that's what you get for being so pretty. Why are you running so fast? There is no one in this side street. It is deserted because it is Sunday and everyone has run away from the chaos of the explosion. In the distance we can hear the sirens and then the shattering of more glass. I saw you, he says again. He is a small man. Yes. He is a small man. What did he see? His breath smells of garlic and wine and he is alone, unsteady on his feet. I know what I see. I take the knife from his back pocket while he waves his baton drunkenly. I am four hours old. In my four-hour life I have bombed a café and now I fight with a policeman. The daisy dress is busting at the seams as my arms and fists hit out at his baby face and I slide the knife across his throat. It is so easy, like drawing with chalk across a blackboard.

Rabah Rabah Rabah

'Yasmina!' I look straight up into the distressed eyes of Doctor Paranoid.

He is whispering now, holding my waist with one arm, looking for something in his trouser pocket with the other, wiping my shins.

'Listen to me.'

No No No.

'Keep your voice down.' He spits on the handkerchief and wipes my face. 'I am going to carry you. Pretend you are one of the wounded from the explosion.'

But I am wounded. Why must I pretend?

'If we are stopped that is what happened. You were wounded in the café and I am taking you to my surgery.' He lifts me, cradles me like a child and carries me to his car, an old yellow Citroën that smells of antiseptic. Stern-faced, he drives in silence through the streets, towards his house.

Streets have been cordoned off. Crowds gather and are dispersed by the army. Firemen are hosing blood stains off the pavement. Bodies with their faces covered in newspaper lie in the gutter. Fragments of glass are being swept into piles as stretchers are carried to ambulances parked nearby. A gendarme waves his arms at the car. The doctor curses, slowing down as the gendarme taps with his knuckles on the window. Doctor P is speaking to him, and I lie in the back, bloody and silent, looking out of the window. Who is that man in the dark suit bending on one knee at the feet of a young woman? He is a doctor. A stethoscope on her heart. He stands up and shakes his head. Someone covers her face in newspaper. And then he stares straight through me, the stethoscope still hanging from his neck. His eyes move over to Doctor P. They nod to each other as he walks over to the window where Doctor P is talking to the gendarme. He explains that he is treating some of the wounded in his surgery. The gendarme nods and waves him on.

'Wait a minute.' Clean Hands puts his head through the window.

'Let me examine her, Pierre. She looks bad.'

'Minor cuts from the glass,' Doctor P replies. 'She just needs tetanus and bandaging.'

Clean Hands points to the ambulances waiting. 'I don't want her to lose more blood,' he says. 'The ambulance will be quicker than your car.'

'I know her parents,' Doctor P tries again. 'It is better that they know she is safe. Nothing serious.' He revs the engine.

'It is my informed opinion,' Clean Hands will not let go, he is a dog with stolen meat, 'that the patient is losing blood. Let me examine her.'

He opens the door and holds out his plump hand to help me. I get out and he looks at me, taking his time, from my sandals up to my bloody shins, lingering for a while on the watch on my wrist and then forcing himself into my eyes. His face is full of thought when he eventually puts the stethoscope over the blood-stained daisy nearest my breast. 'So,' his mouth is close to my ear, 'sorry to hear about your uncle.' The metal of his stethoscope pressing into my chest and he enjoying the fear he can hear in my body. The gendarme comes up to him.

'Take the number of the Citroën and wave him off!' Clean Hands shouts to him. The young policeman looks bewildered, but he notes the number plate all the same and walks over to the car. They are arguing. Doctor P is refusing to move off. The young boy lifts his hands in resignation and walks over to help the men carrying stretchers.

Clean Hands shines a small torch into my right eye.

'Just checking to see if there's any glass,' he says, 'not good if splinters get into the retina.' His plump fingers move on to my left eye.

'You know how you find a rat?' he whispers.

The French word for an Arab hunt or killing is *ratonnade*.

'How?'

'You smell him,' he says, exaggerating the word 'smell,' tapping his nose, as he makes me open my eye, close my eye, open, close.

'Better get back to your friend Pierre Paranoid.' He smiles.

'See you both later.'

19

I love you.

That is what I said to Doctor P. When Clean Hands sent the officers to get me we had just heard that the library had been set on fire. I love you, I said for the second time in our short encounter and my eyes ran from the black smoke of burning books. He was packing medicines into a box to give to the son of a doctor from the countryside. Pharmacists would not sell them to Algerians so they had to be smuggled into people's homes and clinics to treat the wounded. Anti-tetanus vaccine, antibiotics, sterile cotton and penicillin. Packed and ready to go. We were just about to eat chicken and he had bought us two cakes wrapped in a sheet of *Le Monde*.

'You don't want me,' Doctor P replied. 'You want a parent.'

They took him away. And they took me away.

PART THREE

20

The sky is a grey block, low on the flat land. A long drive leads up to the entrance of the château and, on the left, a small farm. After she had laid the first fire for the tourists' arrival, the farmer's wife never returned to the château. They can make their own fires. Her husband chops wood and delivers it to the house once a week, refusing invitations to eat and drink with the tourists. Remind me how many of them there are this year, his wife asks him for the fifth time. He massages salt into the cut in his hand to disinfect it and his eyes water as he speaks. Polish, Italian, German, North African, American, French and English.

Ah, Italian, his wife replies and smiles at the Inspector's wife who sits in the kitchen, stirring lumps of sugar into her coffee.

Poor woman, the farmer thinks, and quickly walks out of the kitchen because he does not like to see her bruised eyes.

The frozen flat fields and thin silver trees are harsh on the eye. There is nothing fecund, luscious, plentiful to relieve the bleak winter scene. The postbox rusting next to the gate is always empty. The blue-green cedars that line the drive have no smell. The foxes that dart across the mud fields are lean and hungry. No one has taken away the black bin-liner full of rotten eggs at the end of the drive, nor the dead rat crawling with maggots in the bin; not even the foxes have gnawed the bare bones of the turkey carcass left over from the Christmas feast. During the day a few lone cars pass the château on their way to Paris, but mostly the roads are empty. This particular morning, even the birds are silent.

The American woman stands in her white nightdress, a glass of milk in her hand, staring out at a field full of black crows. She looks like a child housewife, except the Algerian knows she is bleeding underneath all that virginal cotton. Tatiana, the child who is half-German, half-Italian, takes off her paper crown and examines the patch of dried glue where the glitter has fallen off. She does not look directly at the American woman, but secretly counts the buttons on her white nightdress instead. Tatiana makes one of her pacts with God. If there are twelve buttons on the American woman's nightdress, she, Tatiana, will live a long and happy life. If there are only seven buttons she will die next year, alone in her bedroom in Frankfurt, her mouth full of worms.

The American turns away from the crows towards the Algerian woman, tapping her fingernail against her glass of milk.

'I know Mom shot herself while Sammy and I were asleep. And I know that you found us and stayed with us until the cops found Dad. But how did you know where we lived?'

'She gave me her address. Scribbled on a cigarette pack.'

'Well, thanks a lot, Mom,' the American sneers.

'She wanted me to know where to find her children.'

Tatiana smiles nastily, affecting a mock-American accent, 'I might look the princess, but there's a toad inside me.' She jumps off the chair and runs to the door. 'I want to give you everything I am,' she drawls, and then disappears, shouting something in German to her father upstairs.

'That child's going to end up in a loony bin,' Nancy says distastefully as she pours herself another glass of milk.

'Wilheim wants to know where his wife is.' Yasmina rubs her eyes with the palms of her hands, until she sees a block of deep red in her mind's eye.

Luciana waits patiently for the telephone to ring in the freezing corridor, just as she has done every morning for the past week. Rubbing her bare feet, she sips sparkling mineral water and invents a new fragrance to pass time. Crushed orchids and vanilla. If she was ever to die, she would like to smash her head on the marble curves of a grand sweeping staircase. A cascading fountain nearby. Marble. Orchids. Blood. She suddenly remembers the woman who laid the fire when they first arrived at the château. The farmer's wife lisping on account of her broken front teeth when she came to thank them for the shortbread. She remembers driving Tatiana to the farm because the child wanted to see the goats. Yes. That was the day she saw the sheets drying in the wind outside. Some of them were blood-stained. Great swirls of blood that neither soap nor hot water, nor the will of the farmer's wife could erase from the cotton. The Italian invents a location for another of her fabulous deaths. A hotel overlooking a swollen muddy river. A woman in red satin platform shoes drinks Pepsi-cola. A man appears from the shadows. He wears a straw hat and his pockets are full of rice. He takes out a revolver and places it against her forehead. She presses her lips to his, and it is while they kiss, lip to lip, that he pulls the trigger. When the telephone rings, the Italian realises she is freezing cold and she cannot stop shaking.

'Si?' Luciana drags the telephone cord into the far end of the corridor with dread, staring out at the blue cedars. A shaky woman's voice says, 'This is Louise Blanc returning your call.' The Italian takes in the low grey sky and thinks how small the cedars look against it. She lets in the field to the right of the cedars where an old stallion grazes by the electric fence.

'Are you the woman who sees Horse?' Luciana can hear her stirring sugar into her coffee.

'Yes.'

'Where do you meet?'

'By the port. Where the ferries come in.'

'My husband knows him well. If you can't kick Horse, Horse will kick you.'

Luciana buries her face in her sleeve and takes a deep breath.

'Madame, if you have not found a good surgeon, perhaps I can help you?' Louise Blanc does not reply, but Luciana can hear her conferring with someone else. For a moment she thinks she recognises the voice. What are the right words to describe the kind of torture she knows the ex-military man practises on his wife?

'Madame,' she starts again, 'understand that I will pay your fare to Frankfurt and all other medical expenses.' Another whispering voice intervenes. The Italian knows she has heard it before.

Where? She can sense the woman, the Inspector's wife, preoccupied on the other end of the telephone.

'Luciana?'

'Yes.'

'I am interested in your doctor.'

The Italian is surprised to feel how hard her heart is beating against her towelling bath robe.

'When we meet, Louise, how will I recognise you?'

'I have twelve stitches above my left eyebrow and I always wear blue.' The woman's voice, although tired, is humorous and sardonic. 'You have not answered my question.'

'Ask me again.'

'Why do you want to help me?'

Luciana can feel the pain of blood rushing back into her numb feet. 'I need to talk to you, Madame Blanc, because I am going to have to barter with your husband for my freedom.'

'Did you ever get married, Yasmina?'

Nancy blinks childishly at the older woman, who wants more than anything to go back to bed and sleep.

'My true companion is Safia. We eat together. We teach at the same university. We seek each other's advice and opinion. It is Safia who I describe my life to.'

'I don't have any women friends.' The American plaits and unplaits her mousy hair nervously.

'When we came to England, I put Safia in a clinic. She was badly addicted to certain drugs.' Yasmina puts out her cigarette and stands up. 'She tried to charm her way out, first with the doctors and then with the menial staff, but she came out okay.'

'You know, Yasmina,' the American fiddles with the white lace on her nightdress, 'I'd do anything for love. I'd eat flies.' She sips her milk.

'I kind of hate stories. I feel like you found me and for your own reasons kept in touch and that I have to give you something in return. Like save your life or look after you when you're old. That I have to make some exchange with you and I'm frightened of that.'

'You are quite right. There is something I want you to do.'

Nancy's blue eyes flicker with dread and fear. The clock strikes eleven and they can hear the rest of the house stirring, baths running, shutters opening, the beginning of a new day.

'I want you to kill Mary,' Yasmina says.

'What?' The American frowns in disbelief.

'She is the sacrifice on our island.' The Algerian takes a small penknife out of her pocket. A sharp curved silver blade springs out of the leather sheath. 'We must cleanse the ugly poor English girl with her unsightly white skin from our small community.'

Nancy knows now that this is what she has most secretly feared all along. The blistering rocks and arid desert lands, the squatting robed people with their brutal laws and unfathomable codes, all of this lurking inside the mysteriously self-possessed woman with scars on her stomach.

'Hey, I don't do that stuff.' Nancy shuffles her slippered feet uncomfortably.

Yasmina stares at the American woman for a while and then gathers the silver curls of her head in her hands. After a while she says, 'Only joking.' She wipes her eyes, recovering from some deep hilarity that Nancy, bewildered, does not understand.

'I don't want anything from you.'

The American suddenly feels ashamed and foolish. She glances furtively at the middle-aged academic sitting next to her, spectacles on a cord around her neck. Yasmina has students to teach. Essays to mark. Lectures to prepare. Books to write. This is after all a comfortable château with a well-stocked fridge and cosy log fires, it is not frontline or an underground carpark or city beach or deserted park or mall in the suburbs where someone's psychotic son sprays shoppers with bullets. This is not a place where life is cheap. Her hands are icy cold as she realises Yasmina is saying something to her. She can't hear it all because there is a noise in her head, but she does hear the Algerian say, 'It is not me who is dangerous. It is you who are murderous, cunning and brutal.' She takes out her penknife and starts to peel an orange.

The American watches the coil of peel fall to the floor until the noise inside her fades into a hum. She runs through the hit list in her mousy blonde head. 1. Her mother. 2. Her father. 3. Her husband. 4. Her daughter. Yeah. A bloody early morning massacre. Lucky her ma left her a gun. Her inheritance. Nancy smiles so that the dimples show in her pale peachy cheeks.

'I'm going to make us an omelette with Gruyère.'

21

'We are all Europeans now.' Everyone is eating a late breakfast, and no one wants to talk. Wilheim doesn't care. He nudges his wife's arm. 'Eat for a change, Luciana.'

'I have no appetite.'

The fat man reaches for another piece of toast and grins at Philippe with his mouth full.

'You know that phrase "give bombing a chance?" ' He starts again, provocatively. 'Some nations are just psychopathically violent.' When the telephone rings, the English man jumps up so hastily he drags his chair across the floor. He drops the phone and picks it up again, kicking the chair away.

'Civil wars are the most painful kind of wars,' Wilheim says darkly to Mary, spooning raspberry jam into his mouth straight from the jar.

Pinar?

*

It's a boy. Seven and a quarter pounds. One hour of labour for each pound of flesh. I'm sitting in the hospital with a bag full of pesetas for the telepone.

Is he okay?

He will drive a Yamaha and smoke too much, I know it already. He's beautiful. Can you hear him sucking?

No. Yes. Yes! And you?

Not even one stitch. We cried. The doctors and the midwife cried. He cried. He bawled.

What have you called him?

Robert. My father's name.

And mine!

No? Ben, you're joking. Your father's name is Robert?

Yes. Except in English you pronounce the t.

That's good then, isn't it?

I feel like phoning him.

*

Don't be ridiculous.

I know.

Don't even think about it.

I can't help it.

What did I say to you that time?

You said how very kind of you to let a stranger stay the night.

Mary cannot take her eyes off Wilheim. She does not want to see him in detail, she just wants a surface to think on. Something she has known secretly for a long time has suddenly made itself overtly known to her at this moment, and she is not quite sure what to do with the knowledge. Without taking her eyes off the blur of Wilheim's face, his jaws moving, the flash of blue where his eyes are, she goes over the conversation she has just heard – from Ben's point of view. Pinar? Is he okay? No. Yes. Yes! And you? What have you called him? And mine! Yes. Except in English you pronounce the t. I feel like phoning him. I know. I can't help it. What did I say to you that time?

'How very kind of you to let a stranger stay the night,' Pinar Lopez casually remarks to Ben as he carries her small red suitcase up the stairs of his London home. 'Yes, it is,' he replies, opening the window, smiling at her. He finds a bottle of wine while she washes her hands over the sink. 'I could stay in a hotel,' she says. The cork sounds energetic and ripe, too noisy as he whisks it out of the bottle. 'But you don't need to. I have a spare room.' They drink the wine and she takes out a packet of pistachio nuts from her suitcase. When they crack the shells between their teeth, the sound is amplified; he thinks of cicadas chirping in a bush, or of a branch cracking in the countryside at night. He is completely at ease with this Spanish woman he does not know. When she asked him for directions, a map in her gloved hand, and said, 'I am in London for five days and I don't like my hotel,' it was the gloves that struck him as endearing. He said, 'I don't want to sleep with you and I have a partner, but if you want to stay in my house you can.'

She replied, 'Do you have clean towels?'

Now he finishes his wine and picks up his car keys. 'I'm going to the cinema with Mary, have a bath and there are towels in the cupboard.'

When he returns, she is asleep, and he feels comforted by her presence in his house. The bottle of herb shampoo, the electric toothbrush and spearmint paste she has put in his bathroom comfort him. Her hairbrush and the thought of her breathing between the sheets he had washed the day before, and ironed, with her in mind, please him. When Mary asked him if he wanted to stay at hers after the cinema he replied, too quickly – I have a guest, it would be rude – and drove home, happy and excited.

The next day he is still happy and excited, frying bacon and eggs and whistling a new tune. When Pinar Lopez sees him frying eggs for her, she puts her arms around his waist and they can't help themselves. She is dark. He is fair. She comes from there. He comes from here. They like each other. It is an easy and lovely lust, they know how to touch each other and when he the English man cries out with pleasure, lying on the stranger's olive belly, playing with her long black hair, he feels like he is in his favourite place, the salt marshlands on the edge of the Camargue where gulls drop crab claws from the sky and silver fish leap from the shallow waters on to the salt flats. While they fuck the telephone rings and Mary leaves messages on the ansaphone: 'Ben, this is Mary. I've run out of money. Can you lend me ten pounds until Friday? Please call me back.' And they hear the sound of the kisses she blows down the machine, while their kisses, Ben's and Pinar Lopez's, are extravagant, his fingers in her mouth as the machine clicks and whirs and stores messages that he is not going to listen to. Afterwards they drink coffee and eat cakes and she says, 'I have a château in Normandy. You can stay there any time.'

'With you?' He smiles.

'No. I live in Spain with my husband.'

Congratulations, Pinar, the English man exclaims stiffly, and suddenly everyone at the table shouts out their good wishes.

'It's a boy,' he tells them, and then,

Phone soon. We all wish you well here. Bye.

Ben walks back to the table. He lingers behind Mary for a moment and then puts his arms around her shoulders. When he kisses her cheek, lightly massaging her neck, she pushes him away. Philippe breaks his croissant and dips it into his coffee. 'It's nice, a bit of affection, no?' he says harshly to the English woman.

In the next room, the princess stands on a chair in her torn froth of multicoloured taffeta waving her wand. Claudine bows at her feet while Tatiana speaks to her subjects:

'Angels hold up the columns of my parliament. A brass giraffe stands in my garden. Ghosts dance inside the walls of my palace. The black dog dribbles. A castrato sings "When the swallows return from Capistrano" by the grand piano. A blue cat licks its paws. I feed peacocks to the white winged horses in my stables. I go to the cinema to have conversations with my prince. He is called Michael. We hose down the kitchens after we kiss. I wear knitted stockings. He shows me pictures of himself. He was a policeman in Mussolini's army. I trample the roses and violets and wasps with the heels of my silver sandals. I sleep like a bone. The sky is full of constellations I've never seen before. Down, Claudine. The earth is turning and we should be on our heads.'

Claudine bends over and shows her bottom to Tatiana. 'This is my cuckoo,' she giggles. She rubs her eyes twenty-one times and chants 'witch, skeleton, morte.' When she opens her eyes she screams and shakes her ankle bracelet made from sea-shells. 'What shall I paint?'

'A hornet,' Princess Tatiana commands.

*

Claudine draws an onion. Boats with balloons. Ten blue chairs. A giant sunflower bursting into spiders. When the doorbell rings the girls race into the tiled hallway and tug at the lock of the heavy oak door.

'Who is it?'

A fifteen-year-old boy, wearing an old man's suit, stares at the girls. He shuffles his scuffed shoes and eventually says falteringly, 'Pinar Lopez?'

'She lives in Spain.' Tatiana watches his brown hands dig into his jacket pockets.

'Pinar Lopez. You call her.'

'She's had a baby.' Claudine hides behind the princess.

The boy nods. 'I come for my sister.'

Tatiana thinks about the rocking horse in the attic covered with a blanket. She has galloped across her kingdom on that mare many a morning. Just as she has watched the white carved birds hanging on nylon thread fly across the skies of her domain, wondering if they will ever land on earth to feed from the bread she saves for them.

'The name of my sister is Maria. I am her brother.' He fumbles for English words and when Tatiana speaks in German to him he shakes his head nervously.

'Come in,' Tatiana says in French, opening the door wider, and he follows her into the large front room with its fire, its black and white photographs on the wall, and the twelve small ballet shoes arranged on the window-sill.

'He's come for the baby,' Tatiana announces to the bewildered adults.

'What baby?' Nancy gestures to Claudine to come to her, which she does, running across the kelim rugs into her mother's arms. The boy stammers, 'I am looking for Pinar Lopez.'

Ben says, 'She is in Spain. Can I help you?'

'I come to fetch my sister.' He takes out a photograph and passes it to the English man. Ben stares at it and nods, passing the photograph to Philippe who in turn passes it down the table. A brown baby wrapped in a white blanket lies in the arms of a young peasant woman. She is barefoot and leans against the side of a crowded bus, watched by two elderly women from the window as she gazes tenderly into the black eyes of the little girl.

'I come from Mexico. Take Maria home.'

Ben clears his throat. 'I understand,' he says and gestures to the boy to sit down. When the boy does not move the English man says, 'Your sister is sick. She is in a special hospital.'

'Yes. I take her home.'

Ben taps his head. 'Your sister is brain-damaged. Do you understand? Sick here.' He taps his head again.

'I know,' the boy says again. 'I know she is sick.'

'The baby is not here.'

'Pinar Lopez. She pay my mother for baby. I give money back.'

'The girl is not here.'

'Where is she?'

'In a hospital in Paris,' Ben says. 'But I do not have the address.'

'You ask Pinar Lopez?'

Ben looks uncomfortable. Today of all days, he cannot phone Pinar.

Tatiana says, 'Why do you want her?'

'My mother want her.' The boy has lost his stammer.

'But she can't talk or walk or anything.' Tatiana circles him. Wilheim stands up and puts a warning hand on his daughter's shoulder.

The boy says, 'You give me address of hospital in Paris?'

Ben hunches his thin shoulders. 'You give me your telephone number and I will find out for you.'

'No telephone.' He shakes his head.

'Anyway,' Luciana stares vacantly at the boy, 'you can't just walk into the hospital and take her away.'

Monika takes the boy's hand. 'Sit down here,' she says gently, and makes a space for him on the sofa. 'Would you like coffee?' He nods. Wilheim stands up. 'I'll make it.' Luciana's lazy distracted gaze shifts to her husband as the fat man walks to the kitchen, all the while playing with the nugget of silver on her wrist.

Monika talks softly to the boy and he listens, bewildered and uneasy but holding his own all the same, because he interrupts her three times and says the name 'Maria.' Eventually she pauses, and this time she wants to be heard. 'You can have the Gdansk baby. I do not unconditionally love her like your mother loves her vegetable child. So you must have her.' When Wilheim carries the small cup of coffee to the boy, he thanks the German in Spanish. His hand is shaking when he brings the cup to his lips.

'You can have my baby,' Monika says again.

'Polish?'

'I guess so.' She looks bored and malevolent. 'I don't know what her father was.'

The boy stands up, ready to leave, arms folded across the faded grey cloth of his jacket while she writes down her grandmother's address.

She gives it to him and says something in broken Spanish about paying his fare to Gdansk.

'Poland?' He says the word as if she has suggested Mars.

'You must telephone!' she shouts, watching him walk down the drive towards the cedars.

'How's he going to get home?' Luciana's eyes wander across the walls of the room and fix on one place, her body limp and golden.

Monika smiles at the Italian woman. An angry sad twisting of her thin lips. 'He came from nowhere. He came from the dark. Like my baby.' She turns to Ben. 'The Mexican child is dead. My daughter is alive.'

'Brain-dead,' Ben snaps back, irritated. The rash on his cheek glows, an electric stripe of distress.

'Kaput. Finished,' Monika insists.

Luciana makes her eyes disappear into the wall, her fingers rhythmically and relentlessly stroking her bracelet.

Tatiana stiffens her jaw, assuming the blank face and neutral voice of a news reader. 'The little girl is holding her own. The worst is nearly over. She is in all our prayers.'

Claudine starts to cry and Nancy carries her out of the room, scowling at Tatiana.

'She can't help being clever,' Wilheim apologises.

'Don't be absurd, Monika,' Mary shouts at the Polish woman. 'The boy wants his sister.'

'The Mexican woman can have my Sophia with pleasure.' Monika walks towards the door in her low-heeled shoes.

'Her condition is getting worse,' Tatiana formally announces to the room. 'She is in the intensive care unit and her parents are unavailable for comment.' The eleven-year-old girl lifts up her princess dress and dabs her eyes in a parody of grand tragedy. 'She is in a critical and unstable condition. The doctors have done all they can. Goodnight.'

22

'Look.' Inspector Blanc bangs his fist on the Formica desk in his office. 'We now have the results of the autopsy. The English woman died of an overdose of heroin.' He runs his fingers through his new haircut. 'You foolish woman. I know who your contact is. I know Professor Horse better than you do.' When the Italian woman shrugs nonchalantly, Blanc lets his mind wander for a couple of seconds. He suspects one of his sideburns has been shaved a little shorter than the other and worries it will reveal the red mole on his left temple.

Lowering his voice, he leans back in his chair, annoyed. 'We drink with him. We eat crêpes with him. Horse works with us.'

'So what?' Luciana says again.

'Where did Mary get the drug from?'

'I gave it to her.'

'Of course. Why?'

'She wanted it.'

Blanc shuffles the papers in front of him. He is sweating, even though it has begun to snow and the grass outside is covered in fine grey ice. The Italian woman plays with the silver rings on her long fingers.

'Are you going to pump my stomach full of water and string me up naked, Inspector?'

'I'm going to do a lot worse than that.'

'I want to make a statement.' He notes that her voice trembles slightly. Her black feathered gloves have fallen under a chair, and although this worries her, she does not seem to have the stamina to pick them up. Instead, she languidly strokes the cluster of milky gemstones on the most elaborate of her rings. Blanc presses a button on his tape recorder.

'Go ahead,' he encourages her.

'We all decided to play Murder in the Dark.'

'Whose suggestion was it?'

'The English man's.'

'Thank you. Continue.'

'I asked everyone to wait for me before we started. I badly needed to shoot up, as we say in hausfrau circles.'

'Hausfrau circles?'

'We like to get right out of it, Inspector. Right out of Frankfurt, you know?'

He nods.

'Our husbands play golf and our children get chicken pox and the supermarkets order a new brand of something and the stores struggle to meet their sales targets. The jewellers and delicatessens and meat boutiques.' The Italian stops for a moment. It is the first time Blanc has seen her look remotely troubled.

'And the porcelain shepherdesses and Alsatian specialities.'

He notices that she is wearing one of her glittering hairnets: a superstar without a camera, a president without a parliament, she is rock 'n' roll without a microphone.

'So you went upstairs to inject the drugs you bought from Horse.' Blanc glances at the tape recorder.

'Yes. Mary followed me.'

'Why?'

'She wanted to die.'

The Inspector leans back and sighs. He hates the bourgeois with their melodramas and long baths. His mother had to heat up the water and wash in front of the fire, always guilty at wasting money on small pleasures.

'The English woman watched me heat up the spoon and take out the needle. She said, can I try it, and I said, yes.'

'I believe you.' Blanc nods in disgust.

'Thing is, Inspector.' She rubs her eyelids delicately. 'Professor Horse let me down. I'm used to cut junk. Salt, milk powder, toilet cleaner, sugar, denture powder, anything that dissolves. Horse was too pure for me. His stuff takes you to the other side. Your world, Inspector. The dead world, the gégène world, the No No No world, and some of us don't come back.' Her mutant German-Italian intonation is dark, harsh under the solo strip of fluorescent light that sometimes flickers above her rhinestone hairnet. 'Like you, Inspector. You're way down there with us.'

Blanc concentrates on tensing the knuckles on both his hands, deep in thought.

'So the English woman wanted heroin?'

'Oh yes.'

'When you supplied the woman with the drug, was there any-one else present?' Blanc stares out of the window through the slats of his grey plastic blinds.

'No.'

'Thank you.' He gestures for her to continue. She moves the tape recorder closer to her glossed red lips.

'I told her not to shoot it. I begged her – eat it, smoke it, snort it. But she wanted to do it my way. She wanted the works. The next thing I know she dies in the dark.'

Luciana and Blanc sit in silence watching the falling snow.

'I think you understand how serious your involvement in her death is – despite the fact you have refused your right to a law-yer?' Blanc gives his voice a kindly timbre for the benefit of the tape recorder.

'I think you understand, Inspector, that Madame Blanc called me from her hideout. She was very happy to talk to me. I said, Louise, never go back to him. Get well. Your husband lives in hell. He should wear pyjamas, not a uniform.'

'Your coffee, Inspector.' A young policewoman puts her head around the door. When her boss, irritated, shouts something very fast in French, she apologises, spilling the scalding coffee over her wrists in her haste to get away. Luciana lights one of her menthol cigarettes.

'Horse is my sickness, Inspector. We know about yours.'

She flicks her ash on to the acrylic cord of his liver-coloured carpet. Blanc does not reply. Yes. He can feel the red mole under his fingertip. The old barber is losing his touch after all these years. If there is one thing certain to make him crazy, it is an unsatisfactory haircut. He walks over to the filing cabinet and takes a magazine out of the steel drawer. When the Italian woman starts to speak again, he sits down and, frowning, flicks through it.

'We know you prefer playing murder with the lights on, Inspector. So why don't you switch off your tape and tell me what you are going to do?'

The Inspector does just that. He stops the tape and stands up, clicking his thick fingers while he paces the length of his small grey office.

'I think it's Portugal again this year,' he says after a while, turning to the travel brochure he removed from the filing cabinet. He holds it up, pointing to a picture of a rowing-boat piled with fishing nets on the golden sands of a beach.

'I like the sardines. The sea might even be warm enough for a swim. The oranges are the best in the world. They've had their revolution. I'll be too early for the almond blossom but you can't have it all.'

He rubs the two-day-old stubble on his jaw and wearily sits down again.

'Look.' This time he does not bang his fists. 'Is anyone going to cause me problems? The English man? Did he care for her? Will he be difficult and delay my vacation?'

The Italian stares at the first winter snow outside, stroking the brooch she wears pinned to her breast, tiny rubies sculpted into a pair of lips.

'The English man currently shares a bed with Monika.'

Blanc smiles nastily. 'It's the grief, I suppose?' He squeezes the red mole between his finger and thumb.

'I don't care about who loves who.' Luciana's head seems to be shrinking. 'I can't feel anything, Inspector. Junkies don't. Anyhow, Pinar Lopez has just given birth to his baby.'

'Good.' He will never go back to that barber again. The man was clumsy. Had the blade pierced his mole there would have been enough blood for the old man to practise his back stroke in. 'I'd take you out for a pastis but I just don't feel like it.' His smile fades into his jowls. 'What does your husband think of your habit? Presumably he must know?'

'Sure.' She looks so small. Disappearing into the chair. Only her eyes are large in her tiny pin head. It is as if she is being buried alive under the snow.

'He likes it. It suits him. I never raise my voice. I never get annoyed with him. I always look good.'

'Most of his wealth goes into a hole in your arm?'

She yawns, almost invisible. 'For your information.'

'Yes?' He watches the gaze of her turquoise eyes get lost and then settle on the branch of the tree outside.

'She encouraged us to kill her.'

'I don't understand.'

'I told you she wanted to die. She was depressed. She didn't care.'

'I see.' He sighs, thinking about the words 'she was depressed,' 'she didn't care.' The police doctor insisted there was evidence that the victim had struggled and been forcefully held down. Blanc knows a thing or two about depression. When the black dog visits him, it does not just bark at his ankles, it rips them to bone and sinew. The Inspector needs a holiday. When he loosens his tie and stares at the wall, Luciana pretends not to see that something has short-circuited in his dead brown eyes.

'I am going to close the files. But first you must give me the address of my wife's hiding-place.'

The Italian takes a breath. Snow has almost covered the windscreen of her car parked outside.

'To make myself clear to you.' Blanc moves his fingers down to his temple where purple veins pulse angrily beneath his fingertips and Luciana thinks of how the actors who play assassins in the movies always shoot their victims in that place, the side of the head. The man in front of her has become someone else, someone she does not recognise. All the niceties of before, the Madame and Inspector, the cheese and burgundy, the lighting of cigarettes, the flirtatious talk, all that was over. The man rubbing his temples was stronger than her.

'I can either close the file or I can put you away for years.'

She thinks of him now as The Man. He is big. Heavily built. A policeman and soldier. Brawn and muscle packed into the white cotton of his shirt. The Man with the broken head. Luciana almost forgets to breathe out.

'Your wife has moved on of course.' She eventually finds her voice. 'She knew you would trace her.' She watches The Man attempt to interrupt her by once again thrashing his big fists on the desk. She is surprised to be feeling something intensely after all, guessing that it is fear but riding the wave and hearing herself recall some vaguely remembered dreamscape when she says, 'But I will design you a virtual wife. You tell me how you want her to be. You can give her actions and you can give her text. She will say anything you like.'

To her surprise The Man nods. He seems to understand the dreamscape she is trawling through to save her life.

'What would you like her to say?'

'The first thing Louise says is, "I forgive you."' The Man weeps into his hands. 'My wife was fond of brioche,' he tells her in a voice that has scrambled into a mess of fragments.

Luciana buttons up her fake fur chestnut coat. As she shuts the heavy door of his office, she sees him floundering in his head, motionless. A fly caught in honey, she thinks, smiling at the attractive young policewoman who walks briskly past her carrying a pot of coffee, two aspirins and a croissant on a grey plastic tray.

'The Detective Inspector is in urgent need of his mid-morning snack.' The Italian twirls her car keys. 'I don't think he's happy with his new haircut.'

23

The tourists are unsettled after the visit from the Mexican boy.

It is as if his search for the lost child has made each of them more childish. Anxious and vulnerable, they indulge each other's stories. Childhood memories are related with fake bravado as they describe the first time they learnt to swim or bought a liquorice pipe after school. Philippe jokes one night about how he got his first beating from his enraged father. What for? The French man savours the melon-coloured wine in his glass. 'I never used to write on the first line of my school exercise books. I would always start on the second line. My father told me – begin on the first line, that is where the page begins.' He raises his eyebrows and chucks his giggling daughter under the chin. 'But for some reason I could not. I had a horror of the top of the page, it seemed to me right to begin a sentence on the second line. So one afternoon he stripped my school uniform off me, pinned me against the wallpaper of my bedroom – I remember the pattern – little steam trains running through the countryside – and beat my naked butt with the toilet brush.' The French man dissolves into a fit of laughter and then chokes on the exquisite golden wine.

'But Philippe is very close to his father,' Nancy reassures the silent grinning tourists. When Yasmina tells them how she was brought up by her uncle from the age of five, Mary raises her eyes to the ceiling. 'Do you all want the OBE for surviving childhood or something?' Only Luciana remains silent. When probed she says she has no memory of being a child. She thinks she was born a teenager somewhere on the outskirts of Rome, ready to flirt and sweat at her first disco. Monika mutters something about liking the circus and then stops, as if the memory is intolerable.

To break the mood they arrange a concert. Their instruments will be the bird-whistles Philippe gave Nancy for Christmas. The Algerian plays the nightingale-whistle which she fills with water. It warbles like a miracle through the rooms and corridors of the house. Wilheim plays the duck-whistle, harsh little quacking noises. Philippe, dark and small, plays the quail and his American lover plays the sparrow, twittering against the throaty cries of the nightingale. Luciana stoically blows the woodpecker, which needs a lot of breath, the English woman plays the cuckoo, and Polish Monika seems to have chosen a peacock that howls long and hard as if its pride has been wounded. The English man conducts them, hands delicate in the half-light. He brings in one bird after another so that the house becomes an aviary of the loved and loveless, twittering and cooing, screeching and honking, all the while the globe moving across oceans and mountains and eventually into the black ice of a Canadian lake.

*

'Listen to the duck,' Claudine giggles from the TV room. The girls cross their eyes and poke each other as Wilheim gives the whistle his all – it quacks dementedly through the house, drowning out all the other birds.

'He's pathetic.' Tatiana holds the battered old diary from Tangier closer to her face.

'He lets my mother take drugs so she won't ever leave him.'

'If you don't read out loud I'm taking the book back upstairs. It's mine,' Claudine interrupts.

'She's got scabs on her arms.'

'Read it to me.'

'She's going to die and my father is going to let her.'

'Why don't you tell her?'

'My mother doesn't care what I think.'

Tatiana resolves to steal the Tangier diary before she returns to Frankfurt. She will translate it into German and live in a castle in the Black Forest with a white Alsatian dog. She will drink wild strawberry schnapps and eat the best imported peaches from Valencia and she will never wear shoes, not even when it snows. She will collect pine cones barefoot from the forest, and feed them to the fire in her private chamber.

'Read to me,' Claudine insists.

Tangier 1957. So Jim has sex with whores. Tonight he crept into the apartment like he was going to rob the house and I was waiting up for him and I said – I'm going to pieces, Jim.

'The whole universe is in pieces, Janey.'

See, I married a creep.

'Janey, you want equilibrium but it just isn't there. It doesn't exist. There's no such thing. There *is* only disorder, instability, disequilibrium. I mean that's your experience, right?'

I walk towards my husband and I know everything is over. Love is over. Respect is over. Companionship is over. He looks frightened and the words just spill out of me. See here, you dumb fuck, pack your bags and get out of here.

'You're just crazy, Jane,' he says in this sad voice.

So pack your bags, you lying, cheating chicken-brained creep. Pack your bags and go back to America. Play golf and grow a paunch and find yourself some obedient wife with Jesus in her heart and cookies in a tin – get out of here.

'Nothing in the world can hurt me as much as you can, Jane. Honey. I'm stone in love with you. You've blown me away. Since our eyes first met you blew me away. My happiest thing, Jane, is you. My precious. My true love. You are everything. You and me and our kids and all we have made together is everything. There's nothing more important to me than that.'

I play his love words over and over again. Why? 'Cause I guess they're the words I have always wanted a man to say to me. He looks weird, this redhead who was my husband. Like he has this Boy expression on his face while he rolls himself a joint, leaning against the wall, not knowing what to do. The fright in his eyes makes me want to hurt him more, but all of a sudden he's wised up, he's quick on his feet stuffing shirts and books into a bag. Then he's gone.

Gone. All the compromising, kissing, fighting – five minutes and they're gone. I thought of the first time I ever saw a 3-D movie – wearing those polaroid shades and screaming. I thought of the first time I ever hitched a ride with a truck driver in Memphis, the first time I ever tasted a mango and the first time I gave birth. How my water broke and I did everything wrong and held my breath when the contractions started and cried because this was what I was supposed to do better than anything else, push out babies. It seemed like a cruel gift to woman – pain, blood, milk – and the angry tears of new life in her arms.

'They've stopped playing.'

Claudine, her cheeks flushed with the horror of being caught with her grandmother's words, runs with the diary up the stairs. When she sees her father through the crack in the door arranging eight little cognac glasses on the table, she slows down, and even pretends to read more of the book on the top step, just to torture Tatiana who is watching her in disgust. The loved child nonchalantly puts the stolen book back in its hiding-place and then slides down the bannister to count her ballet shoes for the third time that day.

Philippe fills each of the eight small glasses to the brim with Calvados and declares himself wine waiter for the night. The tourists toast each other, clinking glass against glass. The Algerian remarks on the cedars, how they only leak their scent at night and she can smell them now, for the first time.

'That is because you Arabs have long noses.' Philippe smiles.

'That's the kind of thing a jerk like you would say,' Mary turns on him.

Yasmina just shrugs, a faraway look in her eyes.

'Let's play Murder in the Dark,' the English man suggests.

'It's frightening.' Nancy hunches her pink mohair shoulders, all dimples and drunken blue eyes.

'She is a frightened woman.' Philippe puts his arms around his wife and squeezes her hard.

'How do you kill?' Monika inquires in an Ingrid Bergman voice. The English man notices her nipples poking through the black silk of her blouse and finds himself moving closer to her.

'You stroke the victim three times under the chin.'

Monika nods, screwing up her mouth, her pale Polish flesh luminescent every time the flames flicker and climb in the fireplace.

'Under the chin? That's kind of scary,' Nancy complains in a childish voice, nuzzling against Philippe's white polo shirt. 'I don't like the dark.' Mary groans. 'I hate grown-up women who speak in little girls' voices.' Philippe bangs his glass on the table. 'Kill the pig, cut its throat, kill the pig,' he chants and suddenly, Tatiana and Claudine appear, drawn by the French man's chant. They too bang the table and shout in unison, 'Kill the pig, cut its throat, kill the pig, poke its eyes.'

'Are we ready?' the English man shouts above the noise, pouring himself another Calvados.

'Just one minute!' Luciana holds up her hand. 'Wait for me while I go to the toilet.' She runs up the stairs in her red suede shoes with the curved heels and spaghetti-thin ankle straps, untying the silk scarf from her hair. Mary puts down her glass and follows her as the girls shout, 'Kill the pig, cut its throat, kill the pig.'

*

The front door is open and the full moon a fat blue globe in the winter sky. Biddy Ba Ba, who has three small stones tangled in the fur of his belly, decides to purr. He does not stop even when Nancy tries to remove the stones. Claudine holds his back legs and Tatiana his front legs. All three of them lovingly tend to the beast, admiring his long whiskers and the little beard under his tiger chin, the American saying over and over, 'Sorry, Biddy, am I hurting you?'

'Why does Luciana always leave the room like that?' Monika whispers to Yasmina.

'Because she's a junkie.'

'Impossible.'

Yasmina shrugs.

Wilheim puts more wood on the fire. He wants to touch the English woman again. There is something about her unpleasantness that he finds sexy. He wants to excite her body. Knowing that she finds him repulsive excites him even more. He wants to part her thighs and lick her with his tongue until she cries out despite herself, hating him who is so fat and hideous for pleasuring her.

Luciana walks slowly down the stairs. 'Do we all know who the detective is?'

'Yes.'

'So if we are murdered we are stroked three times under the chin?'

'Yes.'

'Ready?' Ben has his hand on the light-switch.

'No.' Mary peers over their heads. She is standing on the third step from the bottom of the stairwell, clutching one of the dark wooden banisters. Wilheim says, 'What is it, Mary?' Everyone is surprised by the tenderness, the familiarity in his voice.

'It is Sunday,' she replies, deadpan.

Ben slides his livid hands deep into his pockets and looks at the floor while his girlfriend mutters something from her place on the stairs, oddly beautiful with her white skin and purple lips. He blocks out her voice, but he knows she is speaking because he can see her lips moving and he can feel the heat of everyone else listening to her. Gradually, he lets in some of her words.

'I was so hungover I drank the holy water from a bowl in the church.' She looks like she's got ice in her veins, Ben observes, and suddenly feels frightened.

'I was thinking about him all the time, like you do. Cherry Shiver they called me on account of my goosepimples. It was exciting. He gave me a golden-winged female lion and we ate Italian cake.' Mary fixes her eyes on the wall, her voice expressionless. 'Eventually I say I'm going to bed. I am in my nightshirt and I am in the kitchen squeezing grapefruits. He comes out of the bathroom and hovers. I say, why don't we listen to music in bed and drink grapefruit rum? He moves towards me and we kiss and nothing is as important as this.'

Ben crosses his fingers inside his pockets to comfort himself. Don't let her frighten you, he cautions himself. I don't know her. Mary is a complete stranger to me and I don't think I like her. He remembers her anger that day when she said, 'We do not come from the same England, you and I.' How he had wanted them to grow old in a garden full of roses, drinking tea sweetened with honey.

'Beautiful kissing. I have been abducted, yeah, I'm so scared.' Mary sighs, stroking her upper lip. 'We're okay. All shook up. It is everything, his hand pressing into my back, see.'

'Gee Mary,' Nancy laughs huskily to herself. 'Who you got in mind for this major experience?'

'Kill the pig. Cut its throat!' the girls scream in unison. Claudine makes her hands into little wiggling pigs' ears and runs away squealing. Ben's cheeks flush as his girlfriend rhapsodises on the stairs. How come this love diva can barely bring herself to kiss him in the morning, pursing her lips shut and staring over his shoulder at the bare branches of winter trees. 'Cut its throat, cut its throat,' Tatiana snorts. Ben grabs a weapon, a cooking pot, and gives it to her to hunt the small piglet running through the echoing corridors of the château.

Monika puts her hand on her ample hip. 'So tell us, Mary, who is your sweetheart?' Luciana taps her curved red heels on the floor.

'That is Mary's secret,' she says harshly in Italian.

Wilheim whispers something to his wife but she just shrugs, pale and golden, shivering in the corridor. When he persists she shouts in Italian, 'If you're so worried, call a doctor!'

The loved and the unloved glance slyly at Luciana. So perfect. So charming. So 'above them all,' Monika thinks once again from the centre of her secret lonely self. The fat German glances up at Mary and then wipes his sweating brow with a dainty plum-coloured hanky. An odd dandyish gesture from the ungainly man with three rolls of fat curving into the back of his neck. 'Mary,' he whispers, and no one knows what to do with the name that echoes through the corridor, so inappropriately mouthed by the fat man.

Luciana gracefully addresses her fellow holiday makers. 'My husband,' she says, 'has an avant-garde way of expressing his cynical view of marriage. He likes to take off his wedding ring and part the thighs of young women. Then he pushes the ring into her sex.'

Philippe laughs. 'Sounds interesting, Wilheim.' He looks around him, quickly noting that his American wife is not amused, but the dark French man is too drunk to censor the guffaws exploding in his throat.

'You might lose the ring, no?' Philippe splutters.

'He always finds it again,' Mary says blankly, and once again, Ben stares at his partner confused. 'Although he is repulsive,' Mary lingers on the word 're-pul-sive' and the German bows his bald head.

She smiles. 'Why don't we play murder now?'

Everyone is relieved when the English man switches off the light and they can hide in the dark. Biddy Ba Ba sits on the stone doorstep staring through the half-open door into the house. Every now and again he bites the stones still tangled in his belly. Scarcely a minute passes before a loud agonised scream sends the cat scampering into a bush. 'AAAAH Murder!' Silence. 'Who is the detective?' someone shouts in the dark over a chaos of footsteps. When the lights are turned on, everyone makes their way towards Yasmina, who is slumped, corpse-like against the wall, clutching her heart.

'I am the detective,' Philippe announces, taking out pen and paper and staring hard at the expressionless faces huddled around the body. He bends down and examines the corpse.

'Yes,' he nods. 'Algerians always die like that.'

'Like what?'

'With a sly smile on their faces.' The French man holds one of Yasmina's ankles in his hands. 'My father said Algerians were easier to kill than rats.'

Yasmina opens her eyes and nods at Monika. 'I told you what people think always finds its way into the world.'

The Polish woman counts the cedars reflected in Yasmina's eyes.

'We've got to find out who did it.' Nancy lights up one of her cigarettes, smoothing her childish plait.

'You did it,' her husband points to her, spilling some more Calvados into his glass and gulping it down thirstily.

'It's not milk, Philippe,' Monika chides.

'Me?' Nancy opens her blue eyes wide. 'No sir. I could not kill a fly.'

The globe moves into Mato Grosso, Chicago, Dallas.

Tatiana crashes into the room and stops abruptly by the body.

'I accuse you, Madame,' the French man once again points to his wife.

'Yes. She did it.' Tatiana agrees.

Nancy throws her cigarette to the floor and stamps on it.

'You are a horrible little girl!' she screams into Tatiana's flushed face.

'Jane-y, Jane-y, can I have some money? What for, Jim? Um. Um. Um. For some candy, Jane-y.' Tatiana looks up at her father just as Nancy swipes her hard across her legs. 'You evil child,' the American chants. 'You evil evil little girl.'

'Gotta codeine, Mama?' Tatiana mocks in a highpitched American accent and then mimes a gun with her two fingers, shooting at the ceiling and making TV bang bang noises in her throat. 'Why don't you just take this gun and put me out of my misery?'

Luciana stares coolly at her daughter. 'Tatiana is a very good actress,' she explains to Nancy. 'I don't know where she gets her lines from.'

'Evil!' the American shouts again, cradling her pastel mohair shoulders with her hands.

'Who is Jane-y?' Monika moves closer to Tatiana.

'She told me.' Tatiana points to Yasmina and glares at Nancy. 'Jane-y, Jim, Safia, Jack, Yasmina, Rabah and Ahmed.'

'What is she talking about?' Wilheim glances at his wife, puzzled. Tatiana shouts at him in German and he suddenly understands.

'You have been telling the child stories?' He smiles conciliatorily at Nancy. Tatiana suddenly bursts into tears. 'Rabah Rabah Rabah,' she wails. When Yasmina rises from the dead and holds Tatiana close in her arms, the assembled tourists witness the strange sight of the eleven-year-old girl weeping as if her world, whatever it is, has truly ended. The middle-aged woman, the North African with scars on her stomach, wraps her arms around the girl, and talks to her in a mixture of Italian, German, English and French. Worst of all, she sobs with her, for a long time, imbued with a grief so private, so utterly removed from them, a grief so big, it is as if the whole château cannot contain its force. Eventually, Yasmina takes a strip of silk out of her pocket and wipes the child's eyes. When Nancy tries to break the charged and terrible silence, the Algerian interrupts her and very seriously thanks the little girl. Thanks her in three languages for her tears, for her curiosity and for her trouble-making spirit. All these things, Yasmina tells the child, are good things, stroking her hair as she buries her face in Rabah's silk handkerchief with its faint lingering scent of roses. Bewildered and embarrassed, everyone begins to look for their glass of Calvados and make small-talk about the tang of apple brandy on the tongue, how it warms the chest and whether it is best to buy it duty-free on the ferry home, or at a local shop.

Philippe puts his hand over the light-switch, shouting out in a bluff, laboured tone, 'Murderers and victims will sort themselves out in the dark,' and turns off the light.

Mary walks barefoot into the living-room with its twelve tiny ballet shoes lined up on the window-sill. She leans her head against the cool stone wall, staring at the black and white photo of the upturned boat on the River Lee, Hackney, vaguely aware of muffled footsteps as people make their way to different parts of the house. She thinks of the taste of the water as the boat turned over and spilled all her passengers into the water. Birds from the local sanctuary circle the floating boat. Mary feels it is her own death, that she is sinking into the weeds of the River Lee, dying among the rusty saucepans and old shoes tangled in the weeds. Drowning under the concrete dust scum that blows from the estates nearby. When something touches her leg she is about to shout out 'Murder' but remembers just in time that the murderer is supposed to stroke the victim under the chin three times. She looks down and sees Biddy Ba Ba rubbing his fur against her bare shins. But there is someone else there, too. Worse, she can see their shadow on the wooden floorboards in the moonlight and she knows she is in danger.

A gentle fluttering of warm breath shivers across the back of her neck. She moves away from it but a hand grips her shoulder and then her breast. It fumbles to feel her bare skin and gives up, moving down to her crotch. Just as the English woman remembers to scream 'Murder' the same hand claps itself over her mouth.

'Bitch,' Philippe drunkenly murmurs into her neck. 'Cold bitch.' The English woman struggles in the dark while he presses her against the wall, opposite the photo of the upturned boat. Claudine, hunched under the window-sill, holds on to the ribbon of one of her twelve ballet shoes. When her father pulls his trousers up and leaves the room she stays where she is, the much-loved child, paralysed under the twelve giant moths that are her dancing shoes. She watches the English woman fall to the floor. Biddy Ba Ba walks in a circle around her. Finally he sits on her stomach, paws tucked under his tiger fur belly, and drifts into sleep. Both cat and English woman look like a perfect picture of repose. They could be lazing by a river-bank on a sunny day, or leaning against a tree, perhaps the tree in one of the photographs on the wall, heavy with blossom and the promise of plenty.

Claudine decides never to dance again. The little girl watches Ben, her godfather, tiptoe into the room. She wants to cry out to him, he who cooks her mushrooms and makes up little tunes for her on his accordion, but for the first time in her life she feels too afraid. When the English man sees Mary he whispers, 'Found you,' bends down and strokes her gently three times under the chin before creeping away to hide in the shadows with Monika. She watches Wilheim, who is out of breath, make his way towards the English sleeping beauty and feel her pulse. He too disappears into the shadows but returns with Luciana, who nods, indifferent to what the fat man is saying to her. The last thing Claudine hears is her mother shouting from some other part of the house, a loud indignant cry, 'Murder, murder!' Claudine tries to get up. She wants to save her mother's life but her small body refuses to move.

24

Monika likes the way the English man kisses her in the shadows. The thin man who holds her tight removes with his kisses the nails from the palms of her hand. Yes. It is time she stopped suffering. It is as if she has been roused from a deathly sleep during which her heart and her country have been turned inside out. Indifferent to her body, grieving for lost love, Monika has slept through centuries. An old peasant woman with a goose under her arm beckons to her in the dark and then fades, like a special effect in a film. The images crowd in as she warms her cold hands under his armpits, totally involved with this theatre of flesh and memory: the two boys in the flat next door who played Jimi Hendrix all day in their bedroom; the four sisters who all slept in the same bed – the very fat one had to sleep at particular fixed times because she did not fit in; the nightwatchman who ran an illegal vodka distillery; the woman downstairs who made sausages and whose sister-in-law was a hairdresser nicknamed the Golden Hand; the trout in the bath fattened up for Christmas. The years of curfew. Of saving dollars. Her five years travelling in Europe with Gustav after he finished studying philosophy at the university in Warsaw. Returning home, loving each other, they visited Auschwitz-Birkenau and bought juice from a vendor in the carpark. When she dug her heel into the earth nearby she retched. The juice was sweet like the smell of death. In the mountains they ate whale blubber ice-cream and swam in the cool mineral waters of the spas. She did not know then, shivering and naked, waiting for him to pass her the towel, that love passes quickly. To be loved and to be abandoned, is that not the way life is? Her daughter would have to agree. Enough snot and tears, Monika thinks. It is time for pleasure. Forget love. Live and yearn. Enjoy good cheese and bread. Choose your friends with care. Stroke small animals that become your companions. Grow old disappointed but laughing.

When they kiss again, it is with all the heat of the uncommitted. Only the cry 'Murder murder' pulls them apart.

'That will be Mary.' The English man grins, and Monika smiles savagely to herself, glad Ben cannot see her for the barbarian she really is.

'Murder' is what she cried into her lonely pillow when she first saw Gustav kissing his young blonde. I have been executed, she thought at the time. For him I no longer exist.

As they make their way to the kitchen, now flooded with light, they can see Nancy lying akimbo on the table, the knitted green tops of her stockings visible under her skirt. 'I'm dead,' she giggles, taking a sip of Calvados, liking the way it burns her lips.

Philippe refills all their glasses, drunk and unsteady on his feet.

'Where is the detective?' His eyes have blurred.

'Here I am.' Wilheim steps forward looking uncharacteristically pale. Tatiana trails behind him, chewing the cuffs of her sleeve.

'So.' Wilheim speaks in a faint distracted voice. 'You, Monika, I think you do not like Americans?'

'You're wrong.' Monika smiles, and everyone thinks for the first time how attractive she is. 'America has long been the yellow brick road to the land of plenty. We have always yearned for America's glistening automobiles to speed us down the highway to somewhere better. No, Sir. We Poles are crazy for Americans.'

'I see.' Wilheim ponders. Nancy lights a Camel Light.

'I hope the corpse is allowed to smoke?' she drawls, leaning on her elbow, and flexing her toes.

'Where is Claudine?'

'Hiding,' Tatiana says. 'Anyway,' she continues, 'I know who did it.'

'Who, mein Liebling?' The detective bends over his daughter and tickles her ear.

'She did it.' Tatiana points to Yasmina.

'Me?' The Algerian makes a puzzled face. 'Why should I want to kill an American?'

'Because she killed you,' Tatiana replies darkly, still sucking the dye out of her cotton cuffs.

'Excuse me, Sir.' The English man steps forward.

'Yes. You have some evidence?'

'I have a query.'

'Speak now or never,' the German insists.

'I believe there are two murderers in this room.'

'On what do you base this assumption?'

'I am one of them.' Ben sticks up his hands in mock surrender. 'But it is not Nancy I murdered.'

Philippe refills everyone's glass. 'Once a wine waiter always a wine waiter,' he sighs. 'Is it time to eat yet?'

'Then who killed Nancy? Because it wasn't me,' Yasmina interrupts.

'I know.' Tatiana walks towards the American.

'Who?' The detective questions her with an extra firm note in his voice.

'She did it herself,' Tatiana says. 'It's suicide. She wants to be like her mother.'

Nancy tenses her mohair shoulders and jumps off the table.

'Where's my daughter?'

'And who did you kill?' Wilheim puts a hand on the English man's shoulder.

'His girlfriend,' Monika volunteers, and stops. The sound of a child crying echoes through the house.

'Maria?' Tatiana makes her eyes wide and rolls them from side to side as the crying gets louder. 'No, it is not Maria. Maria is in hospital in Paris. But she left her white birds and her black horse here.' She turns angrily on Ben. 'You must tell her brother the address so he can take them back to her.' Before he can answer, Tatiana puts her hands together in prayer position and farts. 'Maria kills cats and throws bricks at birds when she goes for walks in the gardens of the hospital. She should be locked up in a cell with criminals. No one has punished her enough. Hurt her.

Then she will know the difference between right and wrong. She's sick. Out of control. Don't let her watch television. Make her cry and then she'll say sorry.' The girl smiles horribly at the bemused adult faces that stare at her. 'No. It is not Maria crying.' She pokes her fingers into her eyes and dribbles. 'It is Sophia. Polish Sophia from Gdansk. She is here. In this house. I can hear her. I hear her every night. She's slicing someone at school with her ruler. She's a liar and a bully and she crawls under the desks and bites the children's ankles. She cuts herself with scissors and pulls out her hair.'

The girl stands on the toes of her patent leather shoes. 'Lock her up. For ever. Don't give her any food. She should be hit until she says sorry. They should take away all her toys until she says sorry. They should set the dogs on her until she says she will be a good girl. She's a liar. Lock her up and throw away the key.' Tatiana runs to the bannisters and turns upside down like a bat. 'Find her. We must find her.'

'Claudine Claudine!' Nancy runs to the living-room where the cries get louder. Philippe follows her. When the American sees Mary sprawled on the ground she is irritated. 'Mary, where's Claudine?' she snaps, distractedly picking up cushions and throwing them on to the floor as if her daughter might be under one of them. The crying gets louder and Mary does not answer. Philippe has just spotted his daughter. 'She's there.' He points under the window-sill, but he does not move. Monika, Ben, Wilheim, Yasmina, Luciana and Tatiana crowd around the English woman while Philippe watches his wife drag Claudine from out of her hiding-place. The golden girl hides her face, sobbing into the soft folds of her mother's pastel mohair jumper.

'What's wrong, sweetheart?' Nancy rocks her daughter, stroking her flushed cheeks. 'Why are you crying?' Philippe watches in terrible sober silence.

'Mary Mary, I've already owned up.' Ben leans over his girlfriend and playfully tickles her ribs. When she does not respond, Monika bends down too and walks her fingers over the English woman's warm blue lips.

'Why has she got bruises on her shins?' Luciana asks in a strained voice. She also looks ill, her immaculate blonde hair damp, darkened with sweat.

'And where's the detective?' Monika is still in a light-hearted mood. She wants to play all night. Wilheim steps forward, his pink face grave and unsmiling. Philippe watches the German lift up the English woman's thin slightly freckled wrist and feel her pulse. Yasmina shakes her grey head. 'It is not possible.' No one knows what she is talking about. 'She is dead,' Yasmina whispers, shocked when Monika laughs. Claudine lifts up her head and peers over her mother's shoulder. 'Biddy Ba Ba killed her,' she informs them all in her sweet girl's voice. Philippe walks towards his daughter and tentatively strokes her nose with his little finger.

'Chérie, I am going to make you supper.' Her father's voice is soft and cajoling. 'What would you like?' When she buries her head in her mother's shoulder, Nancy hugs her daughter and says, 'It's frightening, all these games, isn't it, honey?' Philippe takes his wife's hand and presses his lips to it. Monika is just about to say, 'What a perfect family you are,' but stops because she has just heard Wilheim, who has the telephone clenched under his many chins, ask the operator in broken French to put him through to the nearest police station.

25

Tatiana turns towards Inspector Blanc. 'I know who killed her.'

'Who was it, Princess?' He tries to make his voice careless.

She takes a deep breath. 'You are a man who respects the law, Inspector?'

'Oui, Princess?' Blanc demurs. He feels it is he who is being interrogated and resolves to bring this conversation to an end as soon as he can. He has booked himself on to a flight to Faro in exactly four hours' time and is worried he has over-packed. Are three pairs of shoes excessive for a short winter vacation?

'I want to sue my parents for being born.' The girl has dressed up for the occasion, brushed her hair and scrubbed her hands for an hour with a nailbrush over the bath.

'I know who did it. I want to sue the unloving and make them pay.'

'Tell me, Princess.' Blanc stifles a yawn.

'It is she,' Tatiana points to her mother, 'who murdered me.'

'But you are alive, Mademoiselle.'

'That does not mean I enjoy my life, Sir.' The child rests her chin on her knee.

'Quite so.' The Inspector takes out a cigar. 'But nevertheless you are breathing, little one. You are not on my homicide file and this is not a trial.'

'I pursue my case, Monsieur. I speak English, Italian and German, and I want justice in all three languages. I have been damaged by unlove. It makes me weep at inappropriate moments when I should be dignified. It makes my voice strange and narrows my eyes. My loud laugh has become sly. If I had been loved, I might have had more charm. I might not have been ugly and apologetic. As it is I have only guile.'

The girl gulps for air, clutching her chest. 'She called me evil.' Tatiana spits out the word and cries inconsolably. 'Evil.'

Nancy thinks for the hundredth time that holiday how much she detests, abhors, hates this plump-faced child. How did nature spurt out such a monster?

'I have always cared for you, my daughter.' Wilheim bows his fat head, two tears oozing out of his pale blue pig eyes.

The girl nods at him.

'But all routes lead to Notre-Dame. That means Our Lady The Mother,' she explains to Claudine who stands half-heartedly on the points of her stained ballet shoes. 'I have visited the city of the mother many times. The city of Notre-Dame. It is an old city, paved with cobblestones. It is half-comforting but mostly terrible. The women wear hoods and clogs and watch me from the shadows. I do not want to go there for I am not welcome in that city. I get on a bus and ask for the nearest airport but the driver takes me to Notre-Dame instead. He always does. That is because all routes lead to the mother.'

'You are so dramatic,' Luciana sighs. 'Everything for Tatiana is a melodrama.'

'So you have always said.' Tatiana looks coolly at her mother, whose long legs are crossed on the most comfortable armchair in the room.

'My daughter wants revenge for some crime she feels I have committed. But love is not compulsory. Nor is beauty, of which she has very little. You are wasting your time with me.' Luciana's eyes seem to suck in the colours of the room, now slate grey, now burgundy, her voice matter-of-fact and low, a cool *nouvelle vague* heroine in black petticoat, describing the meaning of life as if reading the instructions on the back of a coffee jar.

'It is a disappointment to me to spawn a child who feels so deeply. I would like to refute the idea that to feel somehow makes you a better person. Who cares? I hope, Tatiana, that in the future you will rip out your womb and pack it with technology. I hope you will completely rewrite the text of your body and that birth will never be your biological destiny as it was mine. I hope you will make your children from a menu that pleases you. Run away now. Take your dirty pointing fingers elsewhere. Go to the TV room and relocate yourself to a simulated city in 3-D. Take control of the water pipes and subways. Placate angry tax payers, disappear into cool grey screens and interact with on-screen actors, interact with concrete, target your enemies with a virus. When you become a politician no one will know you trained on a personal computer. I'm going to cancel all appointments and have a long sleep. I repeat, I have not broken the law.'

'It depends on which law we are talking about.' Tatiana continues to jab her finger at her mother. 'Love is the first and last law. It is the only law worth not breaking. There is nothing else.'

'What we want and what we get are different things.' Luciana is smiling now.

'Yes.' Tatiana turns once again to Inspector Blanc. 'My mother did it. Take her away.'

Blanc looks sideways at Luciana, who gazes into her sheer grey stockings, as if watching TV.

'But it is not you we are talking about, little one.'

The Inspector stubs out his cigar and addresses the English man.

'Monsieur. Is there any detail you would like me to consider before I close my file?'

Ben's fingers tear at the flesh on his elbow.

'I can't remember anything. It's gone. Nothing there.' His voice is anguished and sincere. The Inspector nods sympathetically.

'What is that?'

'Rat blood.' Philippe ambles over to the skirting-board. 'We killed a rat.'

'That is a lot of blood.' Blanc is surprised to find a new note of interest in his voice. Perhaps he should miss his flight after all?

'It was big.' Philippe holds out his hands, describing how large it was for the Inspector. 'It might still be in the bins outside if you want to see.'

'Which one of you killed it?'

'We finished it off.' Philippe smiles, pointing to Ben and himself.

Blanc glances at his watch.

'I think she found me interesting company,' Luciana interrupts in Italian.

'I don't want an interesting mother,' Tatiana replies in German and, despite herself, smiles when she catches Luciana laughing into her gossamer eggshell-blue sleeve.

Nancy strokes her daughter's hair, wondering why it has lost its shine. 'Just before she died, when she talked on the stairs about love and um . . . stuff . . . she kinda looked like she was on the edge of paradise.'

Philippe throws up his hands. 'C'est folie!' he shouts hoarsely, and the Inspector nods in agreement. Encouraged, the French man makes a joke about Detective Inspector Blanc smelling a rat, all the while opening a bottle of champagne with a flourish of the wrist. When he leaves the room, everyone wants him to come back as quickly as possible, missing his panache and good cheer and declaring him champion of the day when he returns with a silver tray laden with iced pale green glasses carved into the shape of lilies.

Biddy Ba Ba sits on the roof of the barn, hypnotised by the snow falling in slow-motion on to the cedars. Where once the agonising vista of open space made his fur rise as he hid behind chairs and under beds, now he wants to be outside for ever. If anything, the frightening place is inside. The danger zones are interiors. Inside is where fearful things happen. Not even snow will force the beast to risk shelter there.

Warmed by the fragrant logs crackling in the stone fireplace, the tourists and the Detective Inspector raise their glasses and toast the New Year, making lists of all the good things they want to happen to them. They joke about losing weight and giving up smoking, careful with each other as they make light-hearted polite conversation, smiling at anecdotes and confessions of weakness.

'I know who killed her,' Tatiana declares once again.

'Who was it, Princess?'

'You did it.' She points to the Inspector.

'You killed her,' she repeats, loudly, in German.

'What does she say?' Blanc looks bemused.

'She says you are the killer,' Yasmina translates in French, and when she does not take her eyes off his puffed face colonised by a network of angry blue veins, the Inspector, who was in the middle of congratulating the French man on his choice of excellent champagne, spills the entire contents of his glass on to his immaculately ironed navy serge trousers.

'Blanc has gone pale,' Luciana whispers deadpan in Italian. When she knows she has her daughter's attention she says, 'I can't remember a thing. It's all gone Blanc.' Despite herself, Tatiana guffaws reluctantly into her hand at her mother's bad joke. Even Claudine, who has decided to be mute for at least three years to make her parents suffer, manages to smile at her friend's infectious laugh. The globe moves into Omsk, Stalino Bay, Baku and finally, when the two girls can no longer conceal their hilarity at the sight of their fathers offering the Detective Inspector an assortment of handkerchiefs to mop himself up, the world stops at Alaska.